Gobble Gobble MURDER

BonzaiMoon Books LLC
Houston, Texas
www.bonzaimoonbooks.com

1

Roland "Beanie" Bean stared at his wife, Noelle, who scowled as she thrust a dirty drinking glass toward him.

At a few minutes after ten o'clock at night, Beanie and the love of his life were in the kitchen, washing dishes. Earlier, following dinner —goat tenders with peas and rice—they'd given their boys, four-year-old Ethan, and two-year-old Evan, baths and then read a few bedtime stories to complete the nightly ritual.

Moments ago, as Beanie scoured a frying pan, he'd mentioned to his wife something he'd forgotten to tell her yesterday. He'd received an invitation to a Thanksgiving get-together hosted by their newest neighbor, a burly man named Eric Barnes. Instead of a formal dinner, Barnes, who'd moved to the Palmchat Islands a year ago and settled in St. Killian, had planned a backyard barbeque. Beanie had been encouraged to bring his family to the casual affair.

Thanksgiving, an American holiday, wasn't celebrated in the Palmchat Islands, but Noelle had gone to high school in the United States when she'd been sent to live with an uncle in Washington, D.C. Beanie had thought his wife might appreciate the chance to celebrate the holiday. Judging from Noelle's crossed arms and the scowl on her pretty face, Beanie had assumed wrong.

"Roland, why on earth would you want to step foot in that … house of horrors?"

"House of horrors?" Beanie shook his head. "Babe, that's a little melodramatic, don't you think?"

"Melodramatic?" Noelle's voice rose an octave.

Beanie winced as he dipped another dirty plate in the sudsy dishwater and scrubbed the ceramic glazed dinnerware.

"Melodramatic?" Noelle repeated. "You think it's melodramatic? You were almost killed in that house."

Beanie ran the clean plate under a stream of tap water and then placed it on the drying rack. "Babe, I wouldn't go that far. I wasn't almost killed—"

"You were viciously attacked by a psychotic—"

"Noelle—"

"No, Roland, don't, okay?" Noelle held up a hand in warning. "Don't pretend that what happened to you in that house wasn't as bad as it was, because you know it was so much worse!"

Exhaling, Beanie said, "Okay, you're right. I did escape with my life that day."

Noelle shuddered. "I don't even want to think about it."

"Elle, despite what happened, I don't see what the problem would be with going to the Thanksgiving party," said Beanie. "The house didn't attack me."

"I know that," snapped Noelle, handing Beanie another glass to wash. "But doesn't that house give you bad memories? I can't drive past it without thinking about what happened."

Beanie submerged the glass in the dishwater.

The peach-colored bungalow several houses down from their own modest home on Dolphin Lane in Oyster Farms had been the scene of a crime Beanie had suffered. The attack he'd experienced was more shocking than traumatic. He'd gone to the house to interview a witness for a story he'd been assigned. As an investigative reporter for the *Palmchat Gazette*, an award-winning Caribbean newspaper, Beanie covered the crime beat. He was used to dealing with sketchy, shady, and often dangerous suspects.

But in the peach bungalow, he hadn't expected to encounter a crazed woman with psychotic tendencies.

Still, he understood his wife's aversion to spending time in the home of the deranged person who'd lunged at him.

"Babe, that's not the house that gives me nightmares," said Beanie, rinsing the glass. "If the new neighbor had moved into Old Wilson's place, I would have turned down the invitation immediately. That's the real house of horrors."

Noelle looked stricken. "House of horrors is an understatement."

Nodding his agreement, Beanie said, "I was talking to Mendez the other day—"

"Mendez?" Noelle frowned. "Why were you talking to him?"

Beanie chuckled. Normally, he went out of his way to avoid Anthony Mendez, their nosy neighbor who lived several houses down. A rapacious gossip, Mendez was prone to spreading unfounded rumors and lurid stories. "He was asking me if I'd heard that Old Wilson's place is for sale and might sell for five, maybe six times its worth."

His wife's formerly stricken expression turned to shock. "Five or six times? That's crazy. Are you serious?"

"Apparently," said Beanie, placing Evan's sippy cup on the drying rack. "There are some real sickos

out there who would love to live in a house where a man who—"

"Mommy! Mommy!"

Attuned to his youngest boy's high-pitched squeak, Beanie turned from the sink. Cute as he could be in his Paw Patrol-printed jammies, little Evan toddled into the kitchen.

"What's the matter, baby?" Noelle sank to her knees, allowing the chubby tyke to run into her arms.

"You okay, bud?" asked Beanie, wondering if Evan wasn't feeling well, or if he'd had a bad dream.

Clapping his hands, little Evan announced, "Mommy, I need to go potty!"

"You need to potty?" Noelle kissed Evan's forehead, then glanced up at Beanie over her shoulder, giving him an excited smile. Recently, Beanie and his wife had stepped up their efforts to potty train Evan, with mixed results. After training Ethan, Beanie figured they would have the procedure down, but Evan hadn't responded to the same techniques. They'd had to be more creative in encouraging Evan to be less dependent on pull-up diapers.

Rising with Evan in her arms, Noelle said, "Okay, baby, we'll go potty."

Beanie asked, "You need me?"

"No, I got it," said Noelle, shifting Evan to her left hip. "You finish the dishes."

"Finish dishes!" echoed Evan. "Daddy finish dishes!"

After tweaking Evan's little nose, Beanie told Noelle, "We'll finish our conversation about Thanksgiving when you get back."

"The conversation about Thanksgiving is finished," Noelle said as she headed out of the kitchen. "I'm not going. And I don't think you should, either."

2

Beneath a low cloud deck with interspersing peeks of sun, Beanie strode up the driveway of 2130 Dolphin Lane, the peach-colored bungalow currently occupied by Eric and Wanda Barnes. Memories of the last time he'd set foot in the house threatened to overwhelm him, but Beanie pushed them away.

Walking along the side of the house, Beanie still wasn't sure how long he would stay at the Thanksgiving party. Two days ago, after Noelle refused to consider accepting the invitation, Beanie had decided to make an appearance, in an effort to be neighborly.

As he approached the half-opened gate, swelling salsa music, cackling laughter, and lively conversation floated in the air.

In the backyard, about fifty people milled around, socializing in clusters as they ate from paper plates and drank Felipe beer, the official brew of the Palmchat Islands. Beanie had expected paper turkey flags strewn between the palm trees or brown and orange balloons, but no festive decorations marked the holiday. Instead, it appeared to be an impromptu backyard gathering. Guests sat on folding chairs and queued up around two long tables set up buffet style against the back fence to partake in Caribbean-inspired twists on traditional American Thanksgiving dishes—stewed plantain casserole, jerk goat legs, peas and rice, Scotch bonnet cornbread, mashed potatoes with sofrito gravy, cornmeal cou-cou, and spicy flat bread.

Eric had told him there would be others from the Oyster Farms community as well as several Dolphin Lane residents, many of whom Beanie knew, and greeted. Soon, he was approached by the host, Eric Barnes, an affable, barrel-chested, boisterous mountain of a man whose gravely drawl could have been intimidating but was instead infectious.

Eric Barnes had struck up a friendly conversation with Beanie a few weeks ago. Barnes had asked about the best way to take care of a Sago palm tree, as he had two flanking the steps leading to his porch. Beanie had provided pointers and learned that Eric had been born in St. Felipe but moved to California with his parents as a kid. Barnes had recounted his rough teen years, and then his stint in the United States Army, which had given him purpose and direction. Beanie hadn't requested Eric's bio, but the guy seemed friendly enough, and maybe eager to prove he wasn't a psycho—unlike the former resident.

"Glad you decided to come!" said Eric.

"Where's your wife and those adorable boys?" asked Wanda, Eric's wife, a petite, curvy woman with a cap of blonde curls. Dressed in short shorts and a V-neck tank top, her glowing coppery tan and ample assets attracted attention from many of the male guests.

Unwilling to admit his wife's aversion to the peach-colored bungalow, Beanie said, "They had a conflicting previous engagement, but they wanted to come."

A blatant little white lie Beanie regretted telling. But he didn't want Eric and Wanda to feel slighted. Beanie understood his wife's reluctance, but the house's tragic past had nothing to do with the Barnes.

"Well, you'll have to fix plates for them before you go," instructed Wanda, her tone somewhat motherly, a stark contrast to her va-va-voom attire.

"Grab a beer and help yourself to some food," encouraged Eric.

"Make sure you try the jerk goat," said Wanda. "Eric was up all last night grilling."

"I will," promised Beanie as Eric and Wanda excused themselves to greet more neighbors.

Deciding he would stay at least thirty minutes, Beanie angled toward the buffet table. He was anxious to taste the jerk goat. Most island locals believed jerk goat could only be properly and authentically prepared by those born *and* raised in the Palmchat Islands. Beanie wanted to test the theory.

Halfway to the table, Beanie heard someone shout his name.

Recognizing the voice, he groaned inwardly. Maybe he could just keep walking to the buffet table. Maybe pretend he hadn't heard—

"Beanie! Hey, Beanie! Over here!"

With a resigned sigh, Beanie glanced toward the right. Anthony Mendez, a George Hamilton doppelgänger dressed in lime green Bermuda shorts, a lemon-yellow polo shirt, and white driving shoes, beckoned for Beanie. Mendez sat at a patio bench beneath a palm tree with four other men, one of whom Beanie recognized, a Dolphin Lane neighbor named Leon Jefferson.

Despite his reluctance, Beanie grabbed a Felipe beer from a cooler on the patio and ambled over to Mendez.

"Beanie, my friend!" said Mendez. "I was hoping you would show up. Where are Noelle and the boys?"

Taking a seat next to Leon, Beanie said, "They made other plans."

"That's too bad, but at least you're here," said Mendez. "And so is Leon. You guys know each other, right?"

"We do," said Beanie, turning toward Leon. "How are you?"

"Doing good," said Leon, taking a sip of beer.

"These three fine blokes are good friends of Eric's," said Mendez, extending his arm to indicate the men he spoke of—a craggy-faced man with a ruddy, sunburned complexion, a dark-skinned man with a wide smile, and a distinguished-looking fifty-something with salt-

and-pepper hair who was dressed like he belonged on a yacht instead of at a backyard get together.

"Aaron, Keith, and Tim," said Mendez.

"Ted …" the fifty-something yachtsman corrected, extending a hand toward Beanie. "Ted Clark."

Beanie shook the man's hand. "Nice to meet you."

Nodding his greetings at the two other men, Beanie shook their hands as well.

Mendez said, "Ted convinced Eric to move back to paradise."

Shaking his head, Ted said, "That was Keith."

Shrugging, the dark-skinned man, Keith, said, "Eric and Wanda had grown tired of London and had been thinking about moving back to the islands, anyway. Wasn't exactly a hard sell."

Mendez said, "Leon's the reason they moved to Oyster Farms."

"Wanda and I work together at Rideaux Bros. Construction," said Leon. "She and Eric were living in Little Turkey. She told me they wanted a bigger place so when this house came up for lease again, I told Wanda."

"Did you also tell her about the previous occupants?" Mendez asked, his eyes glittering with malicious curiosity. "Particularly the wife."

Beanie resisted the urge to roll his eyes.

Leon shook his head. "Didn't know the previous occupants but I heard the husband was killed."

Mendez said, "Well, the wife was a—"

"She had some issues," interrupted Beanie. "But she's getting treatment."

Keith asked, "What kind of treatment?"

Aaron, the ruddy-faced man, asked, "What kind of issues?"

His expression alive with prurient glee, Mendez said, "Well—"

"Excuse me, guys, I'm a bit famished." Beanie stood, not in the mood for Mendez's malicious gossip. "I'm going to head over to the buffet table."

3

"Having a good time?" asked Eric, slapping Beanie on the shoulder.

Surveying the buffet table, Beanie winced slightly. The burly man squeezed his muscles as though he was trying to knead and massage away a persistent knot.

"Having a great time," Beanie said, though that wasn't entirely true. He was having a time, which he wouldn't describe as great. So far, the shindig had been okay, mildly interesting, but he wasn't going to insult his host. In his continued effort to be neighborly, Beanie decided to spare Eric his true opinion. The party was decent but somewhat dull.

"Glad to hear it," said Eric, smiling as he shoved both hands into the pockets of his baggy Bermuda shorts. "And glad the weather cooperated."

Beanie nodded, glancing up at the patches of blue mingling with smoky gray clouds.

"A little humid," said Eric. "But that's to be expected."

"Yeah," said Beanie, reaching for the plastic serving spoon wedged in the mashed stewed plantains.

"So, I was talking to Mendez earlier," said Eric. "He's an interesting fellow."

Beanie chuckled. "Interesting. Hmmm … yeah, that's one word for him."

"He was telling me about the previous renters," said Eric. "A Russian couple. Said the husband was killed."

"Yeah, he was," confirmed Beanie, figuring Mendez had relished the chance to give Eric and his wife the sordid details of their new home's horrific, tragic past.

"Mendez said the wife was a lunatic," said Eric.

Recognizing the not-so-subtle inquiry in his host's tone, Beanie dumped a scoop of mashed plantains on his plate. "Mendez exaggerates. The wife had some … mental issues, but I wouldn't say she was a lunatic."

"Mendez also said that you solved the husband's murder," said Eric, voice lowered. "Is that true?"

Beanie glanced at his host. Eric stared at him, his expression grave and intense. Sensing the man was fishing for a specific purpose, Beanie said, "Well, I wouldn't say I solved the murder. I was able to put some pieces together and figure out who the killer was, but—"

"You work for the *Palmchat Gazette*, right?"

"I'm an investigative reporter," said Beanie.

"Listen …" Eric leaned closer to him. "I might have some pieces I need to put together."

Frowning, Beanie asked, "What do you mean?"

"I don't need to solve a murder," said Eric. "But … there are some mysterious things going on that I need to figure out."

"Mysterious things?" Beanie reached for a grilled jerk goat rib.

"I could use your help," said Eric.

Confused, Beanie asked, "How?"

Eric said, "Follow me into the house …"

After leading Beanie into the kitchen, Eric said, "Take a seat. I'll go get what I need you to check out for me."

Dropping into a chair at the table, Beanie dug into his grub and waited. Mysterious things going on? Something Eric needed him to check out? Beanie sampled the jerk goat and found it rather tasty. As he tried the mashed plantains, his thoughts pivoted back to his host. Obviously, Eric wanted him to investigate something. But, what? And, thought Beanie, why didn't he care?

He was not the least intrigued by the mysterious things going on in Eric Barnes' life. Beanie supposed the man assumed reporters were always interested in the prospect of discovering the truth behind a mystery. To some extent, that was a fair assessment, but Beanie wasn't constantly looking for a reason to snoop. And he absolutely didn't want to get involved in any mysterious goings-on at a house where he'd already experienced more than his fair share of mysterious happenings.

The previous occupants had nearly provided more mystery—and mayhem—than Beanie could handle. But he doubted Eric Barnes' mystery would be more intriguing, or dangerous. He supposed placating his neighbor wouldn't prove too burdensome.

Moments later, Eric returned holding a thick 5-by-7 manila folder in one hand and an unlit cigarette in the other.

"You smoke?" asked Beanie.

Eric scoffed. "Not in the house. And never around Wanda. She thinks I quit. After you and I talk, I'm going to have a quick smoke with Keith. Then I'll have to chew a few packs of gum to get the nicotine off my breath."

Beanie chuckled. "She won't hear anything from me."

"I appreciate that." Eric opened the manila envelope and pulled out several papers, most of them folded in half.

"What's that?" asked Beanie, taking a sip of the guava beer he'd grabbed from a cooler as he'd followed Eric into the house.

"These are the mysterious goings-on I told you about," said Eric, pushing the papers across the table.

Beanie stared at the papers. Why did he get the feeling that Eric had only invited him to the party to discuss the contents of the 5-by-7 manila envelope? The man had done his homework, found out Beanie was a reporter and then decided to solicit his help.

"I've been getting strange emails," said Eric.

"Strange how?" asked Beanie. "Like … threatening?"

"Take a look."

Repressing an exhale, Beanie reached for the emails. He read the first message, which had been sent to ebarnes@palmmail.net from coolkidstable@palmmail.net. The subject line was: *I need answers*. The body of the email, however, was blank.

Frowning, Beanie said, "So there's no message."

"Subject line is the message, I guess," said Eric. "All of the emails have been that way. Just a subject line."

Beanie read the remaining emails, focusing on the subject lines: *I need to know what happened.*

We should talk.

Tell me the truth.

"Have you responded to any of these emails?" asked Beanie.

Eric shook his head. "First, I was too afraid that it was one of those email scams where if you reply, they can steal your identity, or put a virus on your computer. But, as I got more emails from the cool kids table, whatever that is, I started to think that it's somebody who knows me, maybe …"

"Seems like someone who wants information from you," said Beanie, laying the emails back on the table. "They want answers. You have any idea who it could be?"

"None whatsoever," said Eric. "That's why I need your help."

Beanie said, "Maybe you should take these to the police."

"I thought about it, but decided not to," said Eric. "The messages don't seem threatening. Still, I want to know who's sending them."

Beanie rubbed his jaw. "Eric, I have to be honest with you … I'm not sure what I can do."

"Maybe you can—"

A loud two-chord chime reverberated through the kitchen.

Eric exhaled.

Doorbell, thought Beanie as the chime rang out again. And then again, more insistent.

"Someone's at the door," said Beanie.

"Guess I invited more people than I realized." Eric grunted as he stood. "Be right back."

Nodding, Beanie picked up the emails again. The email address was interesting. Cool kids table? Who could that be? Anybody. Someone who knew Eric. Someone who thought Eric could give them answers. *I need to know what happened.* Someone who believed that Eric knew what happened. But, about what? *Tell me the truth.* Again, Beanie wondered, the truth about what?

Beanie scratched his jaw. Maybe it was a weird case of mistaken identity. Maybe Eric Barnes wasn't ebarnes@palmmail.net. Or, rather, maybe the 'e' in 'ebarnes' didn't stand for Eric. Maybe it stood for Eileen. Or Ernie. Or Ephraim. The person who'd sent the emails might have been trying to send them to Elon Barnes. The person might have assumed ebarnes@palmmail.net was Elon Barnes' email and—

"What are you doing here?" Eric's booming baritone flowed into the kitchen.

"We need to talk." A woman's voice, loud, shrill, and angry.

Beanie frowned. Whoever was at the door obviously hadn't been invited.

"I'm busy," said Eric. "In case you didn't realize it, but I'm hosting a party. And I have nothing to say to you, so you can leave."

"I'm not going anywhere until you tell me why you're trying to ruin my life."

Bristling, Beanie winced, wondering if he should get up, or stay where he was. Last thing he wanted was to eavesdrop on a conversation that didn't particularly interest him. But the modest home didn't have soundproof walls and the front door was around the corner down a short hall.

"I'm not ruining your life," said Eric. "You're doing a great job ruining it yourself."

"Is it true you're going to testify against me?"

"I'm testifying for the kids."

"You don't care about those kids," said the woman. "If you did, you wouldn't be helping that jerk take them from me!"

"You don't deserve those kids," Eric said. "I'd be doing them a favor helping that jerk, as you call him, take them from you."

"Eric, please, don't," pleaded the woman. "I know you hate me, but—"

"My testimony has nothing to do with how I feel about you," Eric said. "I am concerned about the welfare of those children."

"I am a good mother!"

"You and I both know that's debatable," said Eric. "But we'll let the judge decide."

"So, I made one mistake and you think I don't deserve my kids?" railed the woman.

"One mistake that could have killed them!"

"Eric, if I lose my kids because of you—"

"You're going to lose your kids," said Eric. "But, not because of me. Because of you."

After a pause, the woman asked, "Do you need another patch?"

"What?"

"For your back," said the woman. "I know it still bothers you."

"My back is fine."

"I can make it better," the woman said. "I'm heading a new project, I can get—"

"I don't need it," said Eric. "I don't want that stuff."

"Then what do you want?" asked the woman. "You want me to

suffer? You want to punish me because I realized you weren't the man I wanted to spend the rest of my life with?"

"Honey, I thank God you came to your senses," said Eric. "If you hadn't, I never would have met the woman I'm going to spend the rest of my life with."

The woman let out a string of bitter, angry curses.

"Get out of my house," demanded Eric.

Seconds later, the door slammed.

Beanie exhaled and reached for his guava beer. He didn't know what to think. Except that he regretted overhearing a tense, fractious conversation that was none of his business. A conversation he couldn't unhear. A conversation that had piqued his curiosity somewhat.

Back in the kitchen, his face flushed, Eric scowled as he yanked a chair from beneath the table and dropped down into it. Beanie glanced at his neighbor. The big man looked drawn and depressed. Despite Eric's bluster and promise to ensure the best outcome possible for the woman's children, his expression was melancholy. Miserable.

"Everything okay?" asked Beanie, to be compassionate and courteous.

"Yeah, it will be." Eric rubbed his jaw and cleared his throat. "Well, I guess you heard that … exchange …"

Beanie said, "Hard not to."

"My voice does carry." After a mirthless chuckle, Eric cleared his throat again. "Anyway, please don't mention to Wanda that my ex-wife showed up."

"That was your ex-wife?" asked Beanie, though he'd figured Eric and the woman had once been in a relationship.

Eric nodded. "Worse mistake of my life."

Beanie said, "Seems as though she feels the same way."

Pinching the bridge of his nose, Eric said, "She's divorcing her current husband—her fourth—and they're in the middle of a nasty custody battle."

"Sounded like, from the conversation, that you're in the middle of it, too."

"Wish I wasn't." Eric exhaled. "But those kids deserve better than her as their mother. I will testify to that."

"Judges tend to be reluctant to separate mothers and children."

Eric said, "I'm going to give the judge a good reason to make sure she doesn't get custody of those kids."

Beanie was curious as to how Eric would manage to convince the judge, but he didn't want to know more about the tense situation than he already did.

Beanie said, "Well … about the emails. I can't make any promises, but I might know someone who can trace them. I'll see what I can find out."

Eric said, "Well, I appreciate anything you can do—"

"Hey, Eric!"

Seconds later, a loud chorus of male voices floated into the kitchen before three men—Eric's friends, Aaron, Ted, and Keith—shuffled into the kitchen.

Waving a lighter and a package of cigarettes, Keith said, "Ready to light it up?"

Snorting, Eric said, "Too bad we're just going to be smoking cigarettes."

Aaron asked, "What do you mean?"

Eric sighed. "I could use something stronger."

Keith asked, "Why's that?"

Beanie figured Eric's ex-wife was the reason for his desire for something more potent to inhale.

Sighing, Eric shook his head. "It's just that … good Lord, Ted, you still have those crazy shoes?" Aaron said, "I told Ted those shoes look ridiculous!"

"Like clown shoes," joked Keith.

Laughing with Aaron, Keith pointed toward Ted's feet. Beanie glanced down, as well. Ted sported a pair of neon green deck shoes. Beanie forced himself not to make a face. The shoes were bad but probably expensive. He recognized the logo. Didn't his co-worker, Stevie Bishop, have a pair?

"I'll have you know that these are bespoke," said Ted, a trace of haughtiness in his tone.

"Be … what?" asked Eric, frowning.

As Aaron and Keith cracked up, Ted tried to explain how exclusive his custom-made footwear was. Feeling like a fifth wheel, Beanie decided to exit, stage left.

"Hey, listen, guys," said Beanie. "I'm going to go back out."

Nodding, Eric said, "Thanks again for your help. And … if Wanda asks, tell her you don't know where I am …"

4

Beanie stepped out of the tiny powder room off the small foyer and paused to check his watch.

How long had he been at the party? Not too long. But definitely long enough.

Following the conversation with his host about the strange anonymous emails he'd received—and the conversation he'd overheard between Eric and his ex-wife—Beanie had returned to the backyard.

After grabbing another Felipe beer, Beanie mingled with other Dolphin street friends and neighbors before making his way back to Mendez. The aging playboy had been in the middle of a story about the exterior security cameras surrounding his home. Thankful that Mendez was no longer discussing the lurid details surrounding the home's former occupants, Beanie listened halfheartedly until nature called.

Beanie strode toward the small study ahead to his right. He was a few feet from the entryway when something caught his eye. A large horizontal mirror above the loveseat. Stopping, Beanie frowned. Wasn't the mirror that caught his eye. It was what he saw in the mirror, from his position in the narrow hallway, that arrested his attention.

Two people standing in front of the window directly across from the mirror.

A man and a woman.

Kissing passionately.

Beanie was confused. Shocked.

The man was his neighbor, Leon. The woman was … Wanda Barnes. Eric's wife. The woman Eric planned to live the rest of his life with, recalled Beanie, remembering the conversation between Eric and his ex-wife. What the …? For a moment, Beanie wondered if he'd had too many beers. Wondered if the mirror was tricking him, reflecting a weird, optical illusion. But, no. Leon and Wanda were kissing. But, why? Beanie mentally chided himself. Wasn't it obvious why? Well, actually, no it wasn't obvious. He had no explanation as to the reason for the kiss, but as a reporter, he regularly assumed and speculated. Employing deductive reasoning, Beanie guessed that Wanda and Leon were having an affair. Or, if not an official affair, then some sort of spur of the moment tryst fueled by insta-lust.

Rubbing his jaw, Beanie wondered if maybe his wife had been right. Maybe attending the Barnes' Thanksgiving shindig had been a mistake. He was still reeling somewhat from the argument between Eric and his ex-wife. And now he'd witnessed Eric's current wife stepping out on him. Geez. What was next? Beanie didn't want to know. He just wanted to—

"Stop. We can't do this." Wanda pushed Leon away. "We'll get caught."

"I don't care," said Leon, pulling her close again. "Maybe he needs to catch us."

"Are you crazy?" Wanda pushed Leon away again. "If Eric catches us, he'll kill us both."

"Not if we kill him first …"

A jolt passed through Beanie. Crossing the hall, he stood against the wall. From his new position, he was no longer able to see Wanda and Leon in the mirror, but he could still hear them talking.

"What did you just say?" demanded Wanda, her tone sharp and shrill.

"You heard me."

"Please tell me you were not serious."

"What if I was?" demanded Leon, a challenge in his tone. "What if I am?"

"You want to kill Eric?"

"I want him out of your life," said Leon. "He doesn't deserve you. And he probably hasn't even been faithful to you."

"What are you talking about?"

"I'm talking about all those trips he took to St. Felipe last year, in April," said Leon.

"You followed him, remember?" said Wanda. "And you found out he wasn't meeting another woman."

"But I didn't find out exactly what he was doing," said Leon.

"Well, he wasn't cheating on me."

"Maybe not then but I'll bet it's only a matter of time," said Leon. "And what does it matter if he's faithful to you? What matters is that he's dead!"

"Do you hear yourself?" Wanda admonished. "Do you really think we could … kill Eric?"

"I think maybe we have to," said Leon. "Maybe that's the only way you can get rid of him."

Rooted to the spot, Beanie was floored. Was he really hearing this? Were Wanda and Leon discussing killing Eric? They weren't serious. They couldn't be. Beanie drug a hand down the side of his face, trying to clear his head. Maybe he'd misinterpreted what they'd said. Maybe—

Beanie's phone chirped, the sound loud and jolting. Wincing, Beanie shoved a hand into the pocket of his pants, yanked out the phone. Fumbling with the device, he managed to silence it.

"What was that?" asked Leon.

Wary of being caught eavesdropping, Beanie hurried back into the bathroom. Glancing at his phone, he read the text from Noelle. *Are you still at the Barnes party? Boys and I are getting takeout. You want something?* Beanie replied, *Still here but getting ready to leave. Getting to go plates so no need for takeout.* Seconds later, Noelle responded, *That's fine. See you soon.*

Beanie sighed. Had Wanda and Leon heard him? Maybe. They must have figured that the sound they'd heard was a phone. But they couldn't have known he was listening. He doubted they would confront him. And maybe his phone had scared them. Maybe they'd scattered. Left the study and scurried back outside.

Beanie took another breath, pocketed his phone, and opened the bathroom door.

Wanda Barnes stood in front of him, staring at him, her gaze shrewd.

"Oh …" Beanie took a step back. "Hi …"

"You okay?" Wanda asked.

Beanie chuckled. "Too many beers."

Wanda's eyes narrowed. Did she believe him? Did she suspect his phone had chirped? That he'd been eavesdropping? Possibly, Beanie conceded. Nevertheless, he doubted Wanda would confront him. And if she did, Beanie would deny listening. He didn't want to think about the disturbing conversation he'd overheard. Didn't want to believe it. All he wanted to do was get out of the house and go home.

Clearing his throat, Beanie asked, "Is Eric out back?"

"Far as I know." Wanda crossed her arms over her chest. "You need him?"

"I wanted to thank him for inviting me," said Beanie. "Tell him I had a good time, but my wife just texted me, so I need to get going."

"Your wife just texted you?"

Too late, Beanie realized his mistake. "Not just now … she texted me before I came into the house and I told her I was going to head home, so …"

"You can't leave now."

"I can't?"

"Eric's going to make a toast. You have to stay for that."

"When is he going to make the toast?" asked Beanie.

"As soon as I make the pitcher of Palmitos," said Wanda, pivoting and walking down the hall.

Following her into the kitchen, Beanie said, "Well, I guess I can stay a few more minutes."

"Did you make to-go plates for your family?" asked Wanda, strolling to the refrigerator. She opened the door, then took out a bottle of pineapple juice, which she placed on the center island.

Standing in the doorway into the kitchen, Beanie said, "Not yet. I was headed out to do that."

Returning to the fridge, Wanda grabbed a bottle of lemonade. "Hope your wife likes the jerk goat."

"I'm sure she will," said Beanie.

Wanda opened the bottle of pineapple juice. "Well, I need to get started on these Palmitos …"

Beanie frowned. "What's the lemonade for?"

"Eric is allergic to pineapples," explained Wanda. "So, I have to make his Palmito with lemonade. Technically, I suppose it's not a Palmito, but … "

"Sort of a modified Palmito," said Beanie.

Wanda stared at him. "Guess you could say that."

Wary of the woman's piercing stare, Beanie managed a quick smile, then excused himself. As he exited the house, he struggled to shake off the apprehension washing over him. Wanda and Leon's disturbing discussion flooded his mind, mixing with Eric and his ex's angry argument. The conversations bothered him, infusing him with a feeling of foreboding unease.

5

"Everybody got a drink?" Eric Barnes' deep baritone boomed across the backyard as the crowd of guests clustered in a semi-circle in front of the buffet tables.

Beanie wiped sweat from the back of his neck. A low cloud deck had floated in from the west, creating overcast conditions but the humidity was still high despite the occasional errant breeze.

"Everybody except you!" called out someone.

Looking from one of his empty hands to the other, Eric laughed.

"Oops! That's my fault!" said Wanda, turning toward the table. She grabbed a red solo cup sitting near a pitcher of the official island cocktail and handed it to Eric. "Here you go, honey! Made this special just for you!"

Claps and cheers broke out.

"Okay, okay, now that we all have a drink," said Eric. "First of all, I want to thank everyone for coming ..."

"Thanks for having us!" Someone in the crowd called out, prompting several other expressions and interjections of gratitude.

Eric continued, "As many of you know, and can probably tell from my American accent, I grew up in the states, even though I was born in St. Felipe. Technically, I'm not an ex-pat—"

"That would be me!" interjected Wanda, looping an arm around Eric's waist.

"And me, too!" someone hollered out.

"And me, three!" said someone else, eliciting hoots and guffaws.

Eric continued, "I've been away from the islands for a long time, maybe too long, and while I was in America, I celebrated lots of American holidays, once of which was Thanksgiving … this is my first time celebrating Thanksgiving in the islands, and I'm thankful for…"

As Eric droned on, taking advantage of a captive audience, Beanie studied the husband and wife. He searched for signs of strife, but their body language conveyed that of a loving couple. *With secrets*, thought Beanie. But their secrets didn't hold the same weight.

Eric's vengeful plotting against his ex was bad but Wanda's cheating was worse. How could the woman stand there, looking adoringly at her husband? Thirty minutes ago, she'd been in the arms of another man. Glancing around, Beanie spotted Leon.

Joking with Eric's friends Keith and Aaron, Leon laughed and shook his head. Beanie was somewhat surprised by Leon's jovial demeanor. But why? Had he expected to find the man skulking off to the side, brooding, and shooting Eric evil, dirty looks? Well, actually, yes. Considering that Leon had suggested to Wanda that they kill Eric. Whether the man had been serious, or not, Beanie didn't know. But joking about murder wasn't funny. Covering the crime beat at the *Palmchat Gazette*, Beanie had seen his fair share of homicide. He knew murder was often preceded by the contemplation of the act. Leon and Wanda had considered getting rid of Eric, which made Beanie wonder if the secret lovers could be capable of—

"Pretty good party, eh," said Mendez.

Somewhat startled by the interruption of his thoughts, Beanie nodded. "Yeah …"

"What do you think about Eric and Wanda?"

Hesitating, Beanie said, "Well … "

Mendez said, "Wasn't sure what to expect but they seem like nice people."

"Yeah," said Beanie, taking a sip of his Palmito, though he didn't necessarily agree, considering the things he'd seen and heard.

Mendez said, "Nothing like the previous renters."

Beanie thought of the young couple whose lives had been marred by strange, tragic circumstances.

"Hey … " said Mendez. "I think something just happened …"

Confused, Beanie glanced at the elderly man, his tanned, leathery skin lined with anxious concern as he craned his neck.

Beanie asked, "What are you talking about—"

A shrill, high-pitched scream sliced through the balmy air, giving Beanie goosebumps. His heart thumped as he glanced around the crowd, wondering what had—

Chaos broke out in the backyard. A cacophony of shouting rose to a fever pitch as the guests surged forward, converging in a tight circle.

"Oh my God!"

"What happened?"

"He collapsed!"

Collapsed? Beanie's heart rate increased as he fought to remain calm as the crowd surged past him. Who had collapsed? He craned his neck, trying to see, to figure out what had caused the sudden commotion.

"We need a doctor!"

"He's had a heart attack!"

" … a stroke!"

" … a seizure!"

"Let me through!"

Beanie stumbled as he was shoved aside by Aaron, who was followed by Ted and Keith. Forcing his way through the throng of guests, Beanie stopped near Ted and Keith, both shouting at the crowd to stand back and make room.

Several feet ahead, lying in the grass, Eric Barnes convulsed, his body jerking violently as foam bubbled from his mouth.

"Do something!" screamed Wanda, on her knees at Eric's side. "Someone call an ambulance! Help him!"

Aaron took a knee in the grass next to Eric and shouted, "Eric! Can you hear me?" while Ted and Keith, along with several other guests, took out their phones. Seconds later, a terrifying buzz of voices reported the medical emergency, describing the scene and demanding that paramedics come at once.

Shaking, Beanie tried to gather his thoughts. What could have happened to Eric? The man appeared to be having a seizure. But why? Was he an epileptic? If not, what might have caused him to—

"Oh, God, he's not breathing!" screamed Wanda, her fingers pressed against Eric's neck. "He doesn't have a pulse! Eric is dead!"

6

"Dead? Are you serious?"

Closing the door on the washing machine, Beanie sighed as he stared at his wife who stared back at him, her pretty face a mask of shock and horror.

"Actually, I'm dead serious."

Noelle scowled. "That's not funny, Roland."

"No, it's not," agreed Beanie, remembering the terrible events that had occurred hours earlier. After Eric Barnes' collapse, an ambulance arrived twenty minutes later. Paramedics determined Eric had passed away. The body was covered with a sheet and wheeled through the murmuring crowd. Sniffing and moaning her shell-shocked grief, Wanda followed, accompanied by Eric's friends Ted, Keith, and Aaron. Whispering words of encouragement, the trio shielded the sudden widow as they left the backyard, leaving behind stunned and shaken guests.

"I knew you shouldn't have gone," said Noelle, opening the dryer. "I'm so glad I didn't let you take the boys. Imagine if Evan had seen another dead body."

Beanie shook his head. "Elle, it's not like Evan even knew he was looking at a dead body. He thought the woman was sleeping."

"From the way you described what happened to Eric, I'm sure Evan would have known that he'd dropped dead," said Noelle, grabbing freshly dried towels from the dryer. "Collapsing and foaming at the mouth? Both Ethan and Evan would have been scared to death! Probably would have given them nightmares."

Beanie grabbed the remaining clothes from the dryer. "Babe, we can't keep the boys isolated and insulated from every bad thing that might happen."

"Look, I know you think I'm a smother," began Noelle, folding a towel.

Trying to temper his growing frustration, Beanie said, "I don't think you're a smother—"

"But, I don't think there is anything wrong with wanting to protect my children from harmful experiences that might cause them irreparable mental trauma."

"Neither do I," said Beanie, miffed at his wife's insinuation that he thought she was being unnecessarily overprotective. "But, Elle, come on … there was no way I could have known that Eric Barnes would drop dead."

Noelle took the towels to the folding table. "So, do you think Wanda and Leon killed Eric?"

Grabbing a towel to fold, Beanie said, "Why would I think that?"

"Eric Barnes' wife is cheating on him and was talking about killing him with her secret lover," said Noelle, folding another towel. "I think they might have done it."

"Babe, I think that's slippery slope logic," said Beanie.

Noelle shot him an annoyed look.

"And, to be fair," said Beanie. "Leon brought up killing Eric, not Wanda."

"Doesn't matter who brought it up," said Noelle. "The fact that she even discussed it with him is horrible."

"Yeah, you're right," said Beanie.

"So how do you think Eric Barnes died?"

"I think Eric might have had a seizure. Or a stroke. I don't know."

"And yet, after Wanda and Leon talked about killing Eric, he collapsed and died," said Noelle. "You think that's a coincidence?"

"I really didn't think about it until … moments ago, but … I don't know. Mendez made some comment about something tainted in Eric's cup. Not that I can believe Mendez."

"What did Mendez say about something tainted in Eric's cup?"

"Before he collapsed, apparently, Eric took a drink of his Palmito," said Beanie. "Which really wasn't a Palmito. Wanda made it with lemonade."

Noelle made a face. "A Palmito with lemonade?"

"Eric was allergic to pineapple," explained Beanie. "I was in the kitchen when Wanda was making the drinks. She grabbed a bottle of lemonade from the refrigerator, and I asked her about it and she told me about Eric's allergy."

"Well, that's convenient."

"What do you mean?" asked Beanie.

"Wanda had to make Eric a special Palmito," said Noelle. "She had the perfect opportunity to slip something in his drink. Something that caused him to collapse and die."

"You think Wanda poisoned Eric?"

"I don't think he had a stroke," said Noelle. "A seizure is possible. But, a seizure is a symptom of poisoning."

Beanie stared attentively at his wife. As a pharmacist, Noelle knew better than he did what might have caused Eric's death.

"Foaming at the mouth and collapsing are also symptoms of poisoning," continued his wife. "But those are also symptoms of a seizure, also."

Beanie sighed. "I guess it's possible that she poisoned him. But is it probable? I don't know."

"But Wanda had a motive," said Noelle. "Cheating wife plotting with her lover."

"Wanda is not the wife I would suspect," said Beanie. "My money would be on the ex. She's got a better motive. Eric's testimony was probably going to result in her losing her kids."

"I suppose I could see a mother being desperate enough to murder to make sure she wasn't separated from her children … but the ex-wife showed up and then left. How could she have killed Eric? He died in the backyard giving a toast. My money would still be on Wanda."

"Well, you know, we don't know why Eric died," reminded Beanie.

"You know what we do know?"

"What's that?" asked Beanie.

"There's something weird about that house."

Beanie said, "Babe, come on … "

"The wives are shady," said Noelle. "And the husbands end up dead."

7

Taking a deep breath, Beanie told himself to calm down as he focused on not losing his temper.

However, he doubted anyone would blame him, considering his current predicament. And certainly, Beanie felt guilty thinking that taking his boys to school was a predicament. But with Ethan whooping and yelling as he ran around the SUV and Evan fighting tooth and nail to avoid being buckled into his car seat, Beanie was almost at his wit's end.

"Ethan, get in the car. Now, please," said Beanie, still wrestling with Evan, who squirmed and banged his fists in protest of Beanie's effort to make sure he was safe. "Evan, bud, let Daddy buckle you in."

"No, car seat, Daddy!" Evan scrunched his cute little face into a grumpy grimace. "No car seat!"

Swiping his damp forehead, Beanie paused to remove his sports jacket and drape it over the door. To make matters worse, it was a hot, humid morning with oppressive, low clouds.

"I don't want to go to school, Daddy!" announced Ethan, continuing his jog around the car.

"You have to go to school," said Beanie, focusing on Evan again.

"But, I don't need to, Daddy!" said Ethan, suspending his sprint around the car to turn a wobbly cartwheel onto the lawn. "I already know how to read!"

"You need to learn more than how to read," said Beanie, finally managing to buckle the strap across Evan, who did his best to unfasten it. "Evan, what's the matter, bud?"

Beanie didn't understand Evan's reluctance and recalcitrance. Usually, he was excited and anxious to go to the Early Childhood Development program where he spent mornings until his grandmother, Noelle's mom, picked him up. Each night, the little tyke came home chattering about all the activities, games, and projects he'd enjoyed.

"I want to get out, Daddy!" said Evan, his lower lip trembling.

"Don't you want to go to ECD?" asked Beanie, using the acronym for the early childhood center.

"I'm Superman, Daddy!" yelled Ethan.

Beanie glanced over his shoulder. Using the sports jacket as a cape, Ethan ran around the yard, pretending he was flying. Exasperated, Beanie shouted, "Get in the car, Ethan! Now!"

"But, Daddy, I have to—"

"Don't make Daddy say it again," said Beanie. "Get in the car!"

"I want to get out!" cried Evan, trying to unbuckle the car seat strap.

Beanie stared at his two-year-old tyrant. "No, you can't get out until—"

"I have to potty, Daddy!" Evan cried. "I want to get out!"

"You have to potty?" Beanie asked, pinching the bridge of his nose. "Are you sure, Bud?"

"Please, Daddy!" Evan wailed. "I have to potty!"

"Okay, okay …" Sighing, Beanie unbuckled Evan, then turned to Ethan. "Come on. We're going back into the house."

"But, why, Daddy?" asked Ethan, frowning.

Hoisting Evan in his arms, Beanie locked the SUV. "Because I said so. Back into the house. Now."

"Okay, Daddy, but you don't have to yell," said Ethan, skipping up the driveway.

In the house, Beanie took Evan into the bathroom while Ethan watched cartoons in the living room.

Ten minutes later, Evan still hadn't used the toilet.

But he had flushed the toilet several times, giggling and clapping his hands as the water swished around the bowl before it was sucked into the drain. After changing Evan's Pull-ups, Beanie tweaked his nose. "Guess you didn't have to potty, after all, huh?"

The little guy laughed, obviously pleased with himself. He'd gotten what he wanted. A trip to the bathroom to flush the toilet. Beanie made a mental note to talk to Noelle about Evan's sly ruse, which was occurring more frequently. Since the potty training had begun, Evan had become a little master manipulator. He often gaslighted his parents, insisting he had to potty when all he wanted was to flush the toilet, one of his favorite things to do.

"Can we go now, Daddy?" asked Ethan, standing in the doorway. "I am going to be tardy, and Ms. Grandberry will be mad!"

"Ms. Cranberry!" said Evan. "Ms. Cranberry!"

"No, Ms. Grandberry, dummy!"

"Ethan, don't call your brother a dummy," admonished Beanie, shocked, and a bit saddened by Ethan's callous insult.

"Sorry, Daddy, but he didn't say my teacher's name right." Ethan pouted. "It is Grandberry."

"Cranberry," said Evan, laughing. "Teacher is a cranberry! Teacher is a cranberry!"

"Apologize to your brother," instructed Beanie, hoping to curtail a potentially bad habit.

"Sorry, Evan …" mumbled Ethan, looking at the floor.

Beanie exhaled. "Come on, back to the car."

Moments later, as he buckled Evan into the car seat, Ethan tugged his pant leg.

"What is it?" asked Beanie, thankful that Evan wasn't putting up a fuss.

"It's the police, Daddy," said Ethan.

"The police?" asked Beanie, distracted by a buckle that didn't seem to want to snap in place.

"Why are they at that house?" asked Ethan. "Are they going to arrest a robber?"

Confused, Beanie glanced over his shoulder.

Two police cars, blue and red lights flashing, were parked in the driveway of the peach bungalow. The Barnes residence. The house where Eric Barnes had dropped dead two days ago. What was going on? Why were the cops at the Barnes house? Had someone tried to break in? Or had there been some other altercation?

Did their presence have something to do with Eric's death? If so, what? Beanie's conversation with Noelle about the possibility of Wanda poisoning her husband came to his mind.

Moments later, Wanda Barnes was marched out of the house in handcuffs.

Ethan looked up at him. "Why are the police putting the lady in the police car?"

"Police car," mimicked Evan. "Police car."

"I'm not sure, bud," said Beanie. "But I'm going to find out."

8

Two hours later, sitting at his small desk in his tiny cubicle at the *Palmchat Gazette*, Beanie called Officer Damon Fields of the St. Killian Police Department. A trusted source, Fields was also a friend Beanie could count on to share information and keep him in the loop.

After several minutes of small talk and catching up, Beanie said, "Reason I'm calling is because I think one of my neighbors got arrested this morning. Her name is Wanda Barnes. You know anything about that?"

Fields said, "The lady who killed her husband."

"The lady who …" Confused, Beanie trailed off. "Wait. What?"

"Janvier arrested Wanda Barnes for the murder of her husband, Eric Barnes."

Beanie was floored. "Eric Barnes was murdered?"

"Looks that way," said Fields.

"I don't understand," said Beanie, turning to his computer. "I thought Eric died from an allergic reaction."

"That's what the paramedics thought, according to their initial report," said Fields. "But when Detective Janvier got the evidence report on the cup Eric Barnes drank from at the party, there were traces of pineapple in the cup."

"Pineapple?" Beanie opened a Word file to begin typing notes. "That doesn't make sense. Eric wouldn't eat pineapple. He was allergic to it."

"That's what his wife told the cops," said Fields. "But she also told the EMS techs that she gave Eric a Palmito and then he collapsed."

"Yeah, she did," said Beanie. "I was there when she gave him the drink."

"You were?"

After explaining that he'd been invited to the Barnes' Thanksgiving shindig, Beanie said, "Actually, I was in the kitchen when Wanda made the Palmito for Eric."

"Why would she make him a Palmito if he was allergic to pineapple?" asked Fields.

Typing notes for the article he was sure his Managing Editor would demand he write, Beanie said, "She didn't. Wanda used lemonade for Eric's Palmito."

"Lemonade?" Fields asked. "Yuck."

"Well, I guess it wasn't really a Palmito," conceded Beanie.

"So you saw her use lemonade in Eric Barnes' drink?" asked Fields.

Beanie tried to remember. "I don't remember if I did, or not."

"Well, not only were traces of pineapple found in the cup Eric Barnes drank from," said Fields. "But Eric's DNA was found on the rim of the cup, which suggests that he drank from it. Prints on the cup belonged to both Eric and Wanda Barnes. The way Janvier sees it, Wanda Barnes gave her husband a Palmito with pineapple juice, which he was allergic to, on purpose."

"What's her motive?" asked Beanie, but as soon as the question was out of his mouth, a memory of the conversation he'd overheard between Wanda and Leon floated into his head. "Never mind. I think I already know."

"What do you mean?" asked Fields.

After telling Fields about Wanda's and Leon's discussion about killing Eric, Beanie said, "Maybe Janvier should know."

"I'll be sure to tell him," said Fields. "Wanda's motive might have been love. Janvier thinks it's money."

"Money?" echoed Beanie.

Fields said, "Wanda took out a million-dollar life insurance policy on Eric a few months ago."

"So maybe Wanda's motive was love and money," suggested Beanie.

"Or the love of money," said Fields. "But I don't know. Janvier is always so quick-draw-McGraw when it comes to arresting someone. Unfortunately, there are no other suspects. Wanda seems to be the only person who might have wanted Eric dead."

"That's not exactly true," said Beanie, and then he told Fields about Eric's beef with his ex-wife, Michelle.

"Janvier should definitely talk to the ex-wife," said Fields. "But will he? Hey, listen, I need to go, but before I do, anyone else you think I should tell Janvier to check out?"

Recalling the conversation he'd been having with Eric in the kitchen at the Thanksgiving party, Beanie said, "Actually, Eric mentioned that he'd been getting some strange emails for the past few weeks. He wanted me to check them out. Now I'm wondering if whoever sent them might have had something to do with his murder."

"Were the emails threatening?"

"Not exactly," said Beanie. "But Eric seemed to think they were. Now, I'm wondering if maybe Janvier should know about the emails."

Fields said, "I'll mention the emails to him. But I have to warn you. I doubt he'll listen."

After his conversation with Fields, Beanie ruminated on the emails. His speculation about the emailer might have been reaching. Most times, he tried not to engage in unfounded speculation, but it wasn't lost on him that hours after Eric shared the threatening emails, the man had dropped dead. Knowing that the police believed Eric had been murdered made the emails seem more ominous.

Beanie stroked his chin. Was he reading too much into the emails? There was only one way to find out. Trace the emails. Find out who'd sent them and finagle an interview. Standing, he walked to the cubicle of his coworker, Stevie Bishop.

"Hey, what's going on?" asked Stevie.

"I was wondering if your cousin could trace an email account for me."

Stevie's cousin, a mysterious, elusive hacker no one at the paper had ever met, had provided invaluable assistance to *Palmchat Gazette* reporters.

"My cousin is out of town," said Stevie.

Disappointment coursed through Beanie. "Out of town?"

"Actually, out of the country," said Stevie. "On the other side of the world."

Beanie was confused. "The other side of the world?"

"Africa."

"What's your cousin doing in Africa?"

"Not sure," said Stevie. "And I don't know when my cousin will be back. Sorry."

"No problem," said Beanie, before returning to his desk. But it was a problem. A big one. Without the help of Stevie's hacker cousin, there was no way he could trace the emails sent to Eric. No way to determine who the sender was, or if the person might have had something to do with Eric's death.

9

"Thank you for agreeing to see me," said Wanda Barnes, gripping the telephone receiver which allowed her to talk to Beanie through the thick double-paned glass, smeared with handprints of previous inmates and visitors.

Beanie stared at Wanda, her skin sallow under the harsh fluorescent lighting. Through the cloudy glass, she looked both incensed and afraid, her red-rimmed eyes were intense. Beanie went back in time, to that horrible moment when he'd visited Noelle in jail after she was arrested for murder.

Despite her insistence that she was fine and her determination to stay hopeful, Noelle's face betrayed her terror. Beanie took a deep breath. He didn't want to dwell on the troubling memories. Didn't want to revisit the anger and helplessness that had nearly consumed him during that awful situation.

Wanda exhibited the same horror, no doubt shocked and devastated by her predicament.

Clearing his throat, Beanie said, "Thank you for talking to me."

Following his conversation with Fields, Beanie contemplated getting a comment from Wanda Barnes for a follow-up to the initial article he'd written about Eric's death—**POLICE BELIEVE WIFE MADE HUSBAND A KILLER COCKTAIL**. But jailhouse interviews were complicated and hard to get. Not all criminals were given the privilege to meet with the media. Those who were cleared to speak with the press had to give permission, and even then, ultimately, the warden had to give his approval.

He'd been surprised to receive a collect call from the jail. And even more shocked when Wanda Barnes came on the line, requesting that he interview her. Beanie agreed immediately. Direct quotes from the accused would help his article trend, but Beanie doubted Wanda would give him anything other than the standard response. He expected she would protest her arrest and proclaim her innocence. She didn't do it. Couldn't have done it. Wouldn't have done it. The cops had the wrong person, Beanie was sure she would tell him. A murderer was loose on the streets.

Wanda said, "I want to tell my story. I am innocent!"

Beanie was inclined to agree. Not because he thought she was incapable of murder. He didn't know her. She could be capable of anything—including murder. And considering the conversation he'd overheard between her and Leon, it was entirely possible that she had killed Eric to collect a large insurance payout.

Beanie was willing to believe in Wanda's innocence because Detective Philippi Janvier had arrested her.

Whenever Detective Janvier arrested someone, Beanie was suspicious.

To say Beanie had beef with Janvier was an understatement. Their relationship was fractious. The animosity between them had begun when the detective had arrested Noelle for a murder she didn't commit.

Since then, Beanie had witnessed Janvier bungle a number of cases as he focused on the wrong suspects and arrested the wrong people.

"I want people to know the truth," said Wanda.

Beanie hoped she'd be honest.

He wanted to ask her about the Palmito she'd given Eric. Had she purposely given him a Palmito made with pineapple juice? Or had it been a horrible accident? A tragic mix-up? Could she have grabbed the wrong cup?

He also wanted to know more about the life insurance policy she'd taken out on Eric. Had she purchased it with the intent of killing Eric and cashing in on his death? Or was she mainly being realistic, insuring her future should anything happen to her husband?

Of course, Beanie planned to come clean about the conversation he'd overheard between her and Leon. He was sure Wanda suspected he'd heard their discussion of killing Eric. Hopefully, she would agree to speak honestly with him.

"What's the truth?" asked Beanie.

"I did not kill Eric," insisted Wanda. "That incompetent island cop is wrong about me. I didn't give Eric a Palmito with pineapple juice. I wouldn't have done that. Eric was allergic to pineapple. I made him a Palmito with lemonade. You were there in the kitchen. You saw me do it."

"I saw you take a bottle of lemonade out of the refrigerator," clarified Beanie. "But I left the kitchen before you made the Palmito."

Wanda scowled. "I made Eric's Palmito with lemonade."

"Eric's DNA was found on the rim of a cup that contained traces of pineapple," pointed out Beanie, recalling the information Fields had given him. "The cup you gave him, which had your fingerprints on it."

"Or maybe it wasn't," challenged Wanda. "Before I gave Eric the drink I made for him, he might have picked up one of the cups, which had pineapple and rum, and maybe he started to take a drink from it, which would account for his DNA on the rim of the cup. But then, he didn't take a drink from that cup because he smelled the pineapple at the last minute. That might be the cups the cops found, which could have been knocked over in the commotion after Eric collapsed."

Dubious of Wanda's story, Beanie said, "Did you tell the police that?"

"Look, I don't expect you to believe me," said Wanda, practically spitting the words through gritted teeth. "The cops don't. Detective Janvier doesn't. And why not? Because I had an insurance policy on my husband? Since when is that a crime?"

"Tell me about the insurance policy," requested Beanie.

"Eric and I took out policies on each other, which I told the detective," explained Wanda. "I didn't buy the policy because I wanted to kill him."

"So, you think Eric died of an allergic reaction?" asked Beanie.

Wanda shook her head. "Eric was murdered. But he didn't die of an allergic reaction that I caused. I tried to tell that idiot Janvier that an allergic reaction would have made Eric wheeze and cough. He wouldn't have been able to breathe. He would have broken out in hives."

Beanie rubbed his jaw, thinking Wanda had a point, though he didn't admit it.

"I know what happens when my husband has an allergic reaction," said Wanda. "His face swells, his throat closes, and he can't breathe. He has an EPI pen. He would have told me to get it but he said nothing. He took a drink and immediately began to convulse before he dropped dead."

Beanie asked, "What do you think happened to him?"

"Eric was poisoned," said Wanda. "Something deadly was in that cup he drank from, but it wasn't pineapple juice. I didn't kill my husband."

"Do you know who might have killed Eric?"

"His ex-wife wanted him dead!"

"His ex-wife?" asked Beanie, recalling the woman he'd heard arguing with Eric.

"Her name is Michelle Reed," said Wanda. "She's psychotic. I tried to tell Janvier about her but he refused to listen. You need to talk to her. Make her tell you the truth. She killed Eric."

"You have any proof of that?"

Exhaling, Wanda said, "You need to talk to Eric's friends."

"His friends?"

"I think you met them at the party," said Wanda. "Ted, Aaron, and Keith. They can tell you how crazy Michelle is. They know she killed him. Please, will you talk to them? Will you help me?"

Clearing his throat, Beanie said, "Wanda, other than outlining your claims of innocence in an article, I really don't see what I can do."

"You can make sure I get justice," said Wanda, her tone beseeching as she leaned closer to the glass. "You can make sure that Eric's ex-wife doesn't get away with murder!"

10

Sitting at the tiny desk in his small cubicle at the *Palmchat Gazette* offices, Beanie took a sip of his last cup of coffee of the day. Thinking about the article he'd written about Wanda Barnes, which his Managing Editor, Vivian Thomas-Bronson was reviewing and probably revising, Beanie stroked his chin.

The article, written several hours ago, when he'd returned from his visit to the St. Killian City Jail, wasn't exactly award-winning journalism, but all the facts were there. Such as they were. Beanie had done his best to inject a hint of intrigue and mystery into the narrative. His tone was never sensationalistic, but he strove for a captivating slant.

In the end, his story was basically a word-for-word rehash of the jailhouse interview. There was one particular detail he hadn't written: Wanda's claim that Eric's ex-wife had killed him. Without proof, he was careful not to cast aspersions on another party, especially when Wanda offered no corroborating evidence. Her suggestion that he talk to Eric's friends, who she claimed would tell him that the ex-wife was psychotic, was akin to deflection, pointing the finger at someone other than herself. Beanie wouldn't allow a suspect to use his platform, or the *Palmchat Gazette*, to create an account in the minds of readers which might, or might not be true until he could verify the narrative.

Recalling Wanda's willingness to speak with him, Beanie was inclined to believe the woman hoped to influence the court of public opinion. Increasingly, people had started to believe the events and incidents they read about online, in digital newspapers, and on social media sites. No doubt, Wanda wanted people to think she'd been falsely arrested, or perhaps framed by her dead husband's vengeful ex-wife. She was trying to present herself as someone to pity, and at the same time root for.

Beanie didn't know if he'd been convinced by Wanda's role as the grieving widow who'd been set up for murder, but his prose in the article had been objective. As always, he presented the facts and allowed readers to make up their own minds, without his opinion or any tongue-in-cheek commentary.

Still, the idea of the jailed current wife pointing the finger at the bitter ex-wife was scandalous. The salacious detail would cause the article to trend, especially if the headline reflected Wanda's accusation. Beanie took another sip of coffee. He was fine with omitting the allegation. Confident that the headline—**WIFE DENIES CAUSING DEADLY ALLERGIC REACTION**—would attract lots of readers.

Wanda's claim was intriguing, Beanie had to admit.

Considering the argument he'd overheard between Eric and his ex-wife—Michelle—he understood why Wanda suspected Michelle. He'd told Noelle he thought the ex-wife was the more likely culprit. The woman was a mother fighting desperately to keep her children. Eric had been determined to make sure Michelle's kids were taken away from her.

Beanie drummed his fingers against his desk. Maybe he should call Eric's friends for an assessment of Michelle. Before leaving the jail, Wanda had given him the contact information for Ted, Aaron, and

Keith. But so what if they told him the ex-wife was psychotic? Their opinions wouldn't be proof of murder. Killers were often crazy, but not all crazy people were killers. Wanda had probably been exaggerating when she'd described Michelle as psychotic. Beanie doubted the woman was certifiable.

And yet, Eric had been adamant about testifying against his ex-wife. He'd made it his mission to make sure Michelle lost her chance to raise her children. But why? Had he really felt Michelle was an unfit mother? Or had Eric been a vengeful ex-husband?

Curious about Eric's ex-wife, Beanie turned to his computer to research the woman, using the public records and vital statistics databases at his disposal.

Nearly half an hour later, Beanie sat back in his chair, glancing at his computer screen. He'd made cursory notes of his findings, which were interesting.

Michelle Ward was a 38-year-old pharmaceutical researcher at Vaughn Pharma. She worked at the company's St. Killian satellite office and lived in Allegra Shores. She'd been married three times before. Her second husband was listed as deceased, as was her third husband, who'd been Eric. Currently, she was in the middle of a contentious divorce with her fourth husband, a banker with whom she shared a five-year-old and a nine-year-old. The kids Eric didn't think she deserved.

Beanie had located a digital copy of the divorce petition, which contained a litany of back-and-forth insults and accusations between Michelle and her soon-to-be ex-husband. The petition linked to a case docket that listed a preliminary custody hearing scheduled for a few weeks from today. When Beanie clicked on the link to find out more about the hearing, he wasn't surprised to discover it had been continued, a legal term that meant the hearing was postponed. Eric's untimely death likely made the continuance necessary. Beanie imagined that Michelle's soon-to-be-ex-husband's lawyers wanted to revisit their strategy now that their star witness Eric was unable to testify against Michelle.

Grabbing the computer mouse, Beanie executed a few clicks to print the notes he'd crafted about Michelle Ward. He wondered if he should request an interview with Eric's ex-wife. Now that her ex-husband was dead, Beanie was curious to know what she thought. Was she upset? Secretly thrilled? Breathing a sigh of relief? Most of all, what would she say in response to Wanda's accusations?

Beanie grabbed his coffee for another sip but found the cup empty.

Groaning, he stood and checked his watch. Half-past five in the evening. At six, he would leave work and head to his mother-in-law's house to pick up the boys. Another cup of coffee before he hit the road wouldn't hurt, he supposed.

11

The next morning, in the *Palmchat Gazette* breakroom, a large, airy space with glass walls that allowed for people watching, clustered around the coffee bar were three of his colleagues, Caleb Olivier, Sophie Carter, and Stevie Bishop, engaged in conversation.

"Beanie, you're going to turn into a cup of coffee," pronounced Sophie, shaking her head.

"There are worse things I could turn into," countered Beanie, grabbing a fresh Styrofoam cup.

"This is what? Your fifth cup? Sixth?" demanded Caleb, holding a mug that said WORLD'S GREATEST REPORTER—a claim Beanie found dubious, considering the old coot's sloppy, shoddy writing.

At one time during his career, Caleb, the most senior journalist at the paper, had been a brilliant reporter, known for his tenacious investigations and scathing social commentary. As time went by, the old grump had become cynical and careless, not bothering to fact check or string together semi-coherent sentences. When Beanie first started at the paper, most of his assignments consisted of rewriting Caleb's drivel.

Stevie said, "Coffee is good for you."

"In moderation," clarified Caleb. "Sometimes too much of a good thing can be bad for you."

"And sometimes, too much of a bad thing can be good for you," said Sophie, her tone sassy as she opened the refrigerator and took out a bottle of water.

"I don't see how too much of a bad thing can be good for you," said Stevie, walking to a table.

"Well, it depends on what the bad thing is," said Sophie. "If it's cigarettes, then no, it won't be good for you. But if it's—"

"Watch your language, young lady," admonished Caleb, joining Stevie and Sophie at the table.

"I didn't even say anything," protested Sophie.

"But you were going to," said Caleb, grunting as he took a seat. "And I suspect it was going to be highly inappropriate."

"Whatever, Caleb." Sophie rolled her eyes and unscrewed the cap from her bottle of water. "I was going to say donuts, for your information."

Chuckling under his breath, Beanie doubted Sophie but said nothing as he added cream and sugar to his coffee.

"So, Beanie, how'd the jailhouse interview go?" asked Stevie.

"As I suspected," said Beanie, grabbing a stirrer before he turned and headed to the table to join his coworkers. "Wanda Barnes says she didn't kill her husband."

"Of course she didn't," said Caleb, tsking his doubt.

"You believe her?"

"Not sure," said Beanie.

"What's the evidence against her?" asked Stevie.

"Her fingerprints are on Eric's cup," said Beanie.

"Maybe Eric didn't drink from that cup," said Sophie.

"But Wanda was passing out the Palmitos," said Beanie.

"Which means her prints are probably on all of the cups," said Caleb.

Beanie nodded. "Still, traces of pineapple were found in the cup

Eric drank from. He was allergic to pineapple, but Wanda says he didn't have an allergic reaction."

"Well, you were there, right?" Caleb's stare was shrewd. "Did you see him break out in hives?"

"Eric Barnes collapsed and started foaming at the mouth," said Beanie.

"Foaming at the mouth?" Caleb shook his head. "Sounds like the man was poisoned."

"Who made the drinks?" asked Stevie.

"Wanda Barnes," said Beanie.

"She made her husband a Palmito knowing he was allergic to pineapple?" asked Sophie.

Beanie said, "Wanda says she made Eric's drink with lemonade."

Sophie made a face. "A Fauxmito?"

"But can she prove she made his drink with lemonade?" asked Caleb.

Beanie said, "I was actually in the kitchen when she started to make the drinks and I saw her take the lemonade out of the refrigerator, but I didn't see her make his drink."

"So, maybe she did make him a real Palmito," said Stevie. "But pineapple has a pretty strong smell. You would think Eric would have smelled it when he raised the cup to his mouth."

Sophie said, "Maybe Eric was drunk and his senses were dulled."

Shrugging, Beanie said, "And everyone was drinking Palmitos. The smell of pineapple was pretty strong in the air."

"Why were you in the kitchen with the wife?" asked Caleb.

Beanie sighed. "I had used the restroom, and when I came out … "

"What?" asked Stevie.

After fortifying himself with a few sips of coffee, Beanie told his colleagues about the conversation he'd overheard between Wanda and Leon before he followed Wanda into the kitchen.

Sophie scoffed. "Well, that sort of makes it seem like Wanda killed Eric."

"She has motive," agreed Stevie.

"And means," said Beanie. "And opportunity. So, as much as I hate to say this, Janvier might have arrested the right person."

"Unless he didn't," disputed Caleb. "You know that man couldn't catch a clue if his life depended on it."

"If it wasn't Wanda, then who was it?" asked Stevie. "She was discussing killing her husband with her secret lover."

"Maybe Leon," suggested Sophie. "The secret lover."

"Or maybe Eric's ex-wife," said Beanie. "That's who Wanda suspects."

"Why?" Stevie asked.

Beanie took another sip of coffee, then said, "Eric was going to testify against his ex-wife, Michelle Ward, in a child custody hearing. Eric planned to tell the judge that Michelle was an unfit mother. She might have lost her kids because of his testimony."

"Seems like the ex-wife might have had motive," said Caleb. "Don't mess with a mother and her children."

"That's also true," said Beanie. "But I don't know …"

"Here's how I see it," said Caleb. "You've heard what Wanda has to say. Maybe you need to talk to Michelle Ward."

12

Following a quick lunch from Loco Goat, his favorite food truck, Beanie left downtown St. Killian and drove west, toward the airport, then to the Vaughn Pharma satellite office in St. Killian.

Two days had passed since his jailhouse interview with Wanda Barnes. Despite Wanda's strong motive for murdering her husband, Beanie couldn't stop thinking about Wanda's accusation against Michelle Ward. Caleb had suggested that Beanie talk to Eric's ex-wife. Considering that the woman had motive, Beanie was inclined to agree.

Still, he wondered if Michelle had opportunity? Or the means to murder her ex-husband?

Michelle Ward had shown up at the Thanksgiving party unannounced, and uninvited. Beanie supposed that could count for opportunity, but as far as he knew, Michelle hadn't entered the house. She hadn't attended the party. Beanie had seen a photo of Michelle on the Vaughn Pharma website. He didn't recall seeing the pale brunette in the backyard. Then again, he hadn't been looking for her. Was it possible that Michelle had crashed the party?

If so, then means was entirely possible. She could have put

something in Eric's drink. But when would she have done it? But could she have pulled it off without anyone noticing? Maybe. People could be oblivious when they were drinking, having a good time, and not expecting anyone to commit a crime. But Michelle's timing would have to have been perfect. She'd had to have known which red plastic cup contained the Fauxmito, as Sophie had called Eric's special drink. And before Wanda grabbed the drink to give to Eric, Michelle would have to have spiked it. Could she have done that?

Beanie wasn't sure, but he wanted to find out.

Or try to, at least. Not that he expected Michelle to confess to him if she had killed Eric, but she might fall for a few of his reporter's tricks. Maybe.

After parking his car in the visitor's lot, Beanie entered the building, encountering a security guard he went to high school with. The large, beefy man, who'd been a star cricket player, allowed Beanie to enter the building, on the strength of their past relationship, and because he enjoyed reading Beanie's articles.

Inside the building, Beanie walked to the receptionist's desk. There he was thrilled to come face to face with a fellow congregant from church. After a few minutes of small talk, Beanie stated his business.

"I was hoping to talk to Michelle Ward," said Beanie. "I think she works in the research department."

"I know Michelle Ward," said the receptionist. "But she's not here today."

Sighing, Beanie tried to temper his disappointment. After getting past security and encountering a friendly face at the reception desk, he should have figured his luck would run out.

"She's missed a lot of days in the past few weeks," said the receptionist, his voice lowered, expression a mask of conspiracy.

"Why is that?" asked Beanie, willing to solicit office gossip.

"Well, she took off some days because her ex-husband passed," said the receptionist.

"That's actually what I was hoping to ask her about," said Beanie.

"I figured that," said the receptionist, his eyes dancing with malicious delight. "She couldn't stand the man."

"She couldn't?"

"They had bad beef," he said. "Worse than the beef she had with her current husband, who she's divorcing, which is why she's missed so many days. She and the current husband are fighting over the kids."

"So what's her beef with the ex-husband?"

The receptionist shrugged. "I'm not sure, but I heard the ex-husband was going to testify for the current husband. That situation is a mess. And on top of that, she almost lost her job."

"Why?"

"I heard she was accused of stealing fentanyl," said the receptionist. "Security and HR couldn't prove it, but several fentanyl patches went missing on her watch."

"Fentanyl patches?" asked Beanie. From what he knew about the drug, fentanyl was a powerful opioid used to manage pain. Nearly one hundred times more potent than morphine, it was also highly addictive. Recalling a story he'd written about a fentanyl overdose last year, he'd been shocked to learn that as little as three milligrams of fentanyl—equivalent to a few grains of salt—could be deadly.

The receptionist nodded. "They're used for pain. That's what she does. Develops pain remedies. Patches, mainly."

Trying to remember why patches seemed familiar to him, Beanie said nothing.

"Anyway, I wouldn't be surprised if she stole the patches and sold them to finance her divorce," said the receptionist. "She is spending every dime she makes trying to keep her kids."

Minutes later, walking back to his car, Beanie reflected on the receptionist's gossip. Normally, he didn't take gossip seriously. But if Michelle was resorting to selling stolen fentanyl to pay for divorce lawyers who were bleeding her dry, she might have come to a desperate conclusion. Maybe she'd thought that the best way to keep her kids was to make sure the man who could take them away from her was dead.

13

"Mr. Bean, it's nice to see you again…"

"Thank you for agreeing to talk to me," said Beanie, staring at Ted Clark, Eric's friend, the dapperly dressed man he'd met at the Thanksgiving party.

"No problem at all," said Ted, stepping back from the door as he opened it wider. "Come on in."

Nodding his thanks, Beanie entered the foyer of the Adagio Bay condo where Ted resided.

"Would you like anything to drink?" asked Ted. "Coffee? Water?"

Following Ted into the expansive living area, Beanie said, "No, I'm good thanks."

After they sat down on couches opposite each other separated by a low coffee table, Ted said, "You said on the phone that you have questions about Eric's death …"

Beanie cleared his throat. "That's right."

When Wanda had suggested he talk to Eric's friends, Beanie had initially resisted the suggestion. After he'd been unable to speak with Michelle Ward, however, Beanie wondered if Eric had discussed his decision to testify against his ex-wife with his good friends. Wanda claimed Eric's friends would know how psychotic Michelle was. Beanie wanted to find out if that was true.

The day before, he'd contacted Ted and requested an interview. He'd explained that he wanted a quote regarding the new developments surrounding Eric's death. The real reason for speaking to Ted was to learn more about Eric's ex-wife. Beanie hoped to slip in a few questions about Michelle. He wanted to know if Ted shared Wanda's opinion about the ex.

Shaking his head, his face grim, Ted said, "I'm not quite sure what I can tell you other than it's a horrible shock, one that I'm having problems coming to terms with. Just doesn't seem real. I can't believe I'm never going to talk to him again."

As Ted looked away, his eyes glistening, Beanie decided to get to the point. "Do you think Wanda killed him?"

Ted exhaled. "No, I don't. And to tell you the truth, I don't even believe Eric was murdered."

"What do you think happened to him?"

"He was allergic to pineapple," said Ted. "And the EMS workers found the cup he'd drank from, which contained pineapple juice. Eric died from a fatal allergic reaction."

"You think Wanda accidentally gave him a Palmito made with pineapple juice?"

Ted nodded. "There were dozens of those red cups set out on the table. Wanda and Eric were passing the drinks out to guests. I figure Wanda intended to give Eric a different drink, but she probably got confused. It was a tragic mistake with devastating results."

"I spoke to Wanda," said Beanie. "She believes Eric was murdered."

Ted looked confused. "She does?"

"She thinks his ex-wife, Michelle Ward, killed him," said Beanie, staring at Ted, searching the man's smooth, tanned face for a reaction. "What do you think about that? Do you know Michelle?"

"I do know her," said Ted. "But I doubt she killed Eric."

"Did you know that Eric was planning to testify against Michelle in her child custody hearing?"

Nodding, Ted said, "I tried to talk him out of it."

"Why?" asked Beanie.

"Because I wasn't sure of his motives," said Ted. "Michelle can be combative and bitter, but she loves her children, and the kids adore her. Eric said he was thinking of what was best for the children, but he might have been trying to get back at Michelle."

"For what?"

"Leaving him," said Ted, with a shrug.

"Why did Eric think Michelle was a bad mother?"

"I asked him, but he didn't want to get into it with me," said Ted. "Probably because I didn't agree with his decision, but he ended up telling me that Michelle was addicted to prescription pain medication."

"Really?"

"That's what Eric claimed," said Ted. "Michelle had fallen off a horse a few years ago and suffered a neck injury which caused her a lot of pain. Eric said she was abusing opioids. He said she put the kids at risk on several occasions. Claimed she'd driven while under the influence."

The disturbing revelations surrounding Michelle Ward's opioid abuse brought to Beanie's mind something he'd heard Eric's ex-wife say, and he asked, "Did Eric have pain issues?"

"Pain issues?" Ted frowned. "Not that I know of. Why do you ask?"

"Well, I just wondered because ..." Beanie trailed off, quickly thinking how to answer Ted's question without admitting he'd been eavesdropping. Though, technically, he supposed maybe he hadn't been listening to the conversation between Eric and Michelle on purpose, so—

"You lying jerk!"

Confused, Beanie jumped slightly as a blurry object sailed past his periphery. Startled, he glanced at Ted as the object hit the man square in the chest, causing him to cry out as the thing bounced off him and landed on the coffee table.

Beanie glanced at the coffee table.

The object was a … deck shoe made of neon green canvas.

The same shoe Ted had worn to the Thanksgiving party, Beanie remembered. The awful shoes Aaron, Keith, and Eric had teased him about.

His expression a mix of embarrassment and chagrin, Ted jumped up. "Beverly—"

"Don't you Beverly me, you dolt!"

Concerned, Beanie glanced over his shoulder.

Dressed in a skimpy sundress, Beverly sauntered toward Ted. Scowling, wobbling on sky-high heels, she pointed a finger in the man's face. "You promised me—"

His complexion crimson, Ted said, "I know, Sweetheart, but—"

"But, nothing!" said Beverly, pushing past Ted as she marched toward the foyer. "You promised me you were going to stop smoking! And what do I find in the guest bedroom? A pack of cigarettes hidden in the closet!"

"Bev, sweetheart, I can explain—"

"I don't want to hear it!" roared Beverly. "If you don't stop smoking, then don't ever expect me to kiss you again because I don't like kissing an ashtray! Now, I'm going to get my nails done. When I come back, I want every cigarette that you have hidden in this house gone!"

Seconds later, the front door slammed.

Beanie jumped.

Ted returned to the couch, his face a mask of humiliation. "Sorry about that. Bev is overdramatic sometimes, but I did promise to—"

"It's no problem," said Beanie, standing, not inclined to become involved in whatever issue there was between Ted and Beverly. "I actually should probably be going. But before I go … "

As Ted walked with Beanie to the door, he said, "Yes …?"

"Wanda wanted me to speak with you because she said you knew that Michelle was psychotic," said Beanie. "Is that true?"

Ted sighed. "I would not say that Michelle is psychotic, but ..."

"But?" prompted Beanie.

"But, maybe I should have said this earlier," said Ted. "I guess I just didn't want to cause anyone any trouble."

"What do you mean?"

"There's a reason why Wanda thinks Michelle killed Eric," said Ted.

"Some other reason besides the fact that she thinks Michelle is crazy?" asked Beanie.

Ted said, "It's because Michelle shot and killed her second husband ..."

14

The next morning, in the pre-dawn hours before the boys woke up, Beanie sat at the kitchen table with Noelle, sipping coffee.

"Are you serious?" asked Noelle. "Michelle Ward shot and killed her second husband?"

As the coffee percolated, Beanie had shared with his wife what he'd learned from Eric's friend, Ted, during their conversation the previous day.

"Well, Ted hadn't known any details," said Beanie. "He heard the story secondhand from Wanda. So, Ted couldn't verify the veracity, but Wanda believed it, hence her theory about Michelle's guilt."

"Wow," said Noelle, bringing the mug of steaming coffee to her lips. "Crazy."

"Yeah, but is it true?" Beanie asked. "And how do I find out? And if I find out it's true, then what does that mean?"

"Just because Michelle killed her second husband doesn't mean she killed Eric," said Noelle.

"Exactly," agreed Beanie. "Still, I wonder why Wanda didn't mention that Michelle had killed her second husband?"

"You would have thought Wanda would have led with that

interesting tidbit," said Noelle. "Anyway, what happened when you went to Vaughn Pharma to talk to Michelle Ward?"

After a sip of coffee, Beanie leaned back in his chair. "I didn't get to talk to her."

"Why not?"

Massaging the back of his neck, Beanie said, "She wasn't at work. The receptionist told me she's missed several days due to her divorce and child custody hearings."

"That's not surprising," said Noelle. "When are you going to try to talk to her again? You have to find out what she thinks about Wanda's accusations."

"I'm not sure, but, if I have any trouble getting an interview with Michelle, Stevie said he would help me out," said Beanie, recalling his coworker's offer, which had been given without a trace of superiority. Thus, Beanie had been robbed of the chance to make a snide remark about Stevie's status as a one-percenter.

Confused, Noelle asked, "How?"

"Stevie's dad plays golf with Vaughn Hines," said Beanie. "The founder and CEO of Vaughn Pharma."

"What's that tone, Roland?" asked Noelle.

"What's what tone?" asked Beanie, trying to sound confused, but he knew what his wife meant. He'd heard the slight resentment in his voice. He knew he shouldn't be salty about Stevie's wealth.

Wasn't Stevie's fault that he'd been born a Bishop. Wasn't Stevie's fault that his family, one of the richest in the world, owned the Felipe Brewing Co., which produced the famous, award-winning Felipe Beer, the official brew of the Palmchat Islands.

"For a moment, you sounded like you were upset that Stevie wanted to help you."

"I wasn't upset," protested Beanie. "I'm not upset. I just don't know why Stevie thinks I would need his help. I've never had any problems getting an interview."

"Well, I know a little bit about Vaughn Hines," said Noelle, sitting her mug on the table. "He's super private, super secretive, and super protective of his company, including his employees, who often have to jump through flaming hoops of fire to please their demanding boss."

"I've heard all about his exacting, critical reputation," said Beanie, reflecting on the reclusive Aerie Islands billionaire.

"It's entirely possible that Michelle Ward would have to ask permission from Vaughn Hines before she can talk to you," said Noelle. "If Stevie can help facilitate the interview, then …"

"I know, I know," said Beanie, remembering the lack of pomposity in Stevie's tone. "Stevie said his father could get Vaughn to tell Michelle to talk to me."

Noelle reached across the table to grab his hand. "Which is a good thing."

Beanie smiled. "Yeah, I know. Considering what I found out about Michelle, I want to interview her."

"What did you find out?"

After sharing with Noelle the gossip given to him by the receptionist at Vaughn Pharma, Beanie said, "Not that I think she killed Eric. But, you never know."

"You think Wanda did it?" asked Noelle.

Beanie shook his head.

Noelle asked, "Then who?"

"I agree with Ted," said Beanie. "It was a horrible accident."

Shrugging, Noelle said, "Unless maybe it wasn't …"

15

Three hours later, after dropping the boys off at Noelle's mom's house in Handweg, Beanie sat at the small desk in his tiny cubicle at the *Palmchat Gazette*, typing additional notes from his conversation with Eric's friend, Ted.

He was nearly finished when he heard, "There's been another arrest in the Eric Barnes case."

Recognizing the voice of Vivian Thomas-Bronson, the Managing Editor of the *Palmchat Gazette*, Beanie turned toward his boss, standing in the opening of his cube.

A tawny beauty with sleek braids cascading down her back, Vivian was a former foreign war correspondent who'd worked for the *Washington Post*. After a decade covering wars and insurrections and genocides in Africa, she'd settled down in paradise with her husband, Leo Bronson, owner of the newspaper.

"Another arrest?" asked Beanie.

With curt efficiency, Vivian said, "I've arranged a jailhouse interview for you with the suspect in custody."

Standing, Beanie grabbed his keys. "Who's the suspect?"

When Vivian told him the name, Beanie said, "Janvier arrested him."

Vivian nodded. "For the murder of Eric Barnes."

Beanie asked, "What evidence does Janvier have against him?"

"That's what you need to find out," said Vivian.

"Does this mean that Wanda Barnes is no longer a suspect?"

"That's also on your list of things to find out."

An hour later, Beanie clutched the receiver used to converse with inmates. Through the thick, smeared Plexiglas, he stared at the man.

Leon Jefferson.

Wanda Barnes' secret lover.

"Can you tell me why you were arrested?" asked Beanie, surprised, and yet not shocked that Leon was now behind bars. Hadn't he heard the man discussing the idea of killing Eric?

"It's like I told the detectives," said Leon. "I killed Eric Barnes. I switched the red plastic cups. I knew the cup Wanda had set aside for Eric—"

"The cup with the Palmito made with lemonade instead of pineapple?"

Leon sneered. "The cup that contained lemonade and white rum. Not sure what you call that, but it wasn't a Palmito. Anyway, I switched that cup with the cup Wanda gave me, which was a real Palmito."

"And you deliberately switched the cups?" asked Beanie.

Leon looked away for a moment, and then said, "I wasn't trying to kill him."

"But you knew he was deathly allergic to pineapple," pointed out Beanie.

Exhaling, Leon said, "I thought he might break out in hives and have problems breathing. I wanted him to suffer. I didn't want him to die."

"Are you sure about that?"

Leon's scowl returned. "What do you mean?"

"You wanted Eric dead," said Beanie.

"I wanted Eric out of Wanda's life," insisted Leon. "Listen, I know what you think you heard—"

"I know exactly what I heard."

"So what are you going to do?" asked Leon. "Rat me and Wanda out to the cops?"

Catching the flicker of panic in Leon's gaze, Beanie said, "I doubt what I heard matters now that you've confessed."

Sighing, Leon pressed a thumb against the corner of his eye. "I didn't have a choice. I couldn't let Wanda go down for something I knew she hadn't done."

"So Wanda had nothing to do with it?"

Leon frowned. "Wanda is not a murderer."

"Help me understand something," said Beanie. "If you didn't mean to kill Eric, then why did you propose the idea to Wanda?"

"I didn't mean that I really wanted to hurt the guy," said Leon, his expression contrite. "I just wanted Wanda to see how serious I was about us being together."

"Serious enough to kill her husband?"

Leon sighed. "Eric didn't deserve Wanda, okay? The guy wasn't a saint."

"What do you mean?"

"Eric is dangerous," said Leon. "And Wanda only married him because she was down on her luck and felt she had no other choice."

"What do you mean, Eric is dangerous?" asked Beanie.

"The next time you talk to Wanda—"

"Assuming there is a next time," said Beanie.

"Ask her to tell you about the gun she found hidden in the laundry room," said Leon. "It belonged to Eric. When she showed it to me, I checked it out. Two bullets were missing from the chamber, which means he'd used the gun."

"How do you know the gun belonged to Eric?" asked Beanie. "How do you know Eric fired the weapon?"

Leon scowled. "Well, I know it wasn't Wanda's gun."

"How do you know that?"

"I know because Wanda told me—"

"And how do you know Wanda was telling the truth," said Beanie, wary of secondhand information.

"Wanda didn't lie to me," insisted Leon. "Eric—"

"Time's up," announced a guard, his deep voice abrupt and authoritative.

Annoyed, Beanie asked, "What were you going to say about Eric?"

Leon opened his mouth, but the guard snatched the receiver from him and slammed it down. "When I say time is up, you follow orders, do you understand me?"

Slouching, Leon turned as the guard clamped a meaty hand around his forearm and pulled him away.

16

"Leon didn't kill Eric," insisted Wanda.

"But he confessed," said Beanie, staring at the woman, wondering if she was delusional. Pacing across the living room, Wanda hugged her arms around her chest. Though the charges against her were still pending, she'd been awarded bail. For the past two days, she'd been out of jail, and according to Mendez, telling everyone she could that Leon was innocent.

"I know he told the police he switched the red plastic cups, but—"

"You don't believe him?"

"I'm sure he did it," said Wanda, circling the coffee table.

Sitting on a wicker chair, Beanie looked at Wanda, wary of her furtive eyes and the grim line of her mouth. Dressed in a loose-fitting halter top and dingy white cut-offs, she looked like contents under pressure with her stringy, unkempt hair and smudged make-up.

At any moment, she might explode.

Beanie's stomach twisted.

Being alone in the living room with the wife of a murdered man took him back to the time when he'd been in the company of a different wife whose husband had also been killed. That wife had attacked him. Left him shaken and shell-shocked. Would Wanda do the same? Leap on him and scratch his eyes out?

Beanie shook away the ridiculous thoughts.

Clearing his throat, he asked, "So … if you believe he switched the cups—"

"I already told you," said Wanda, stopping to glare at Beanie. "There was no pineapple in that plastic cup. He didn't have an allergic reaction. He was murdered. Someone poisoned his drink. And Leon didn't do that. He switched the cups, but he didn't poison Eric."

"But don't you think it's possible that Leon accidentally killed Eric?" asked Beanie. "Your husband was allergic to pineapple."

Wanda exhaled. "Yes, but there wasn't enough pineapple juice in the drinks to cause an allergic reaction. I put a lot of rum in those drinks. Mostly rum. Eric's allergy was bad, but not necessarily deadly. He would have had trouble breathing. He wouldn't have collapsed and foamed at the mouth!"

Scratching his chin, Beanie conceded Wanda that point.

"The police are so clueless!" Wanda resumed her pacing. "They don't seem capable of looking at the situation logically."

Beanie said, "Detective Janvier is not interested in logic."

"I'm going to prove that Eric was poisoned," said Wanda. "I've requested an autopsy. The Medical Examiner has a backlog of cases, but I don't care. I'll wait as long as I have to. I'm going to get justice for Eric and make sure Leon doesn't spend the rest of his life in prison."

"Suppose the Medical Examiner concludes that Eric was poisoned," said Beanie. "Would you think Michelle had poisoned him?"

Eyes flashing, Wanda said, "I would know that Michelle poisoned him. She works at Vaughn Pharma. She has access to all sorts of drugs. Chemical compounds that can kill you in ten seconds or less. Stuff that won't show up on a normal toxicology report. You have to be looking for the types of drugs she could get her hands on."

Recalling the Vaughn Pharma receptionist's unsubstantiated

conjecture about Michelle Ward selling fentanyl, Beanie wondered if Wanda might be right.

"But why would Michelle poison Eric with a drug from the pharmaceutical company where she works?" asked Beanie. "The police would be able to trace the drug back to her."

Plopping down on the couch across from Beanie, Wanda tucked her legs beneath her. "Michelle thinks she's smarter than everybody. She probably doesn't think I've got sense enough to get an autopsy so she figures the poison she used will never be discovered."

Beanie asked, "Is there anyone else who could have killed Eric?"

Wanda looked confused. "Like who? And why? Michelle was the only person Eric had beef with."

"But Eric had a gun," said Beanie, recalling what Leon had told him.

"A gun?"

"That's what Leon said," said Beanie. "He told me to ask you about the gun you found in the laundry room."

Wanda waved a dismissive hand. "Eric used that gun for target practice."

"So that's why two bullets were missing from the chamber?"

"Eric was once in the army," said Wanda. "He liked to keep his skills sharp."

"Leon made it seem like there was something more to it," said Beanie.

"Well, there wasn't," said Wanda.

"So, the gun wasn't for protection?"

Wanda frowned. "Is that what Leon said?"

"Not, exactly, but—"

"Look, Leon exaggerates sometimes," said Wanda, rubbing her eyes. "Says things he doesn't mean."

"Like suggesting the two of you kill Eric?"

Untucking her legs, Wanda swung them to the floor and leaned forward. "What if I could prove that Michelle killed Eric?"

"Prove it how?" asked Beanie, skeptical, wary of the manic gleam in Wanda's pale blue eyes.

"Michelle threatened to kill Eric."

"Speaking of that," said Beanie, remembering his conversation with Ted. "Why didn't you tell me Michelle killed her second husband?"

Wanda leaned back. "Thought it would be better if you heard it from someone other than me. Someone with no skin in the game. Didn't want you to think I was making things up. Trying to deflect blame. Michelle already killed one husband. She wouldn't have a problem killing another husband."

"Why did she kill her second husband?"

"I don't know all the details," said Wanda, shaking her head. "But what matters is motive, right? I can prove that Michelle wanted Eric dead. She sent him threatening text messages."

"You have the texts?"

Wanda's face fell. "They're on Eric's phone, which is password protected so I don't know the password, and the cell phone company refuses to give it to me or reset the phone."

"Did you tell the police about the texts?"

"That Janvier idiot is not listening to anything I'm telling him," said Wanda. "The way he sees it, everything I say is just an attempt to lie my way out of a prison sentence."

"Sounds like Janvier," quipped Beanie.

"That's why I need your help," said Wanda. "I need you to keep my story in the paper. Keep the pressure on the police to solve this case so Eric can get justice and Michelle can go to jail where she belongs."

Thinking of Eric's locked cell phone, Beanie said, "I have a better way to help you."

"And what way is that?" asked Wanda, her gaze dubious.

"I might be able to unlock Eric's phone so you can give the police the threatening texts …"

17

Sipping his third coffee of the morning, Beanie stared at his computer screen.

Following his second cup of coffee, which he'd brewed shortly after arriving at work, he'd spent the morning fact-checking articles and making follow-up calls for comments. A few hours later, when the need for another cup of joe arose, he went to the breakroom. Back at his desk, Beanie accessed the metrics for the articles he'd written about the Eric Barnes case. So far, the stories continued to trend, with plenty of daily comments, likes, and shares. Of course, a few trolls showed up to burst his bubble, complaining about his writing and his intellect. Beanie didn't let the distractors bother him. Objective journalism was supposed to illicit a myriad of opinions.

In the paper's morgue database, which housed previously published stories, he pulled up the first article he'd written.

COPS SAY WIFE MADE HUSBAND A KILLER COCKTAIL

At that point, Janvier had been operating on a theory that Wanda Barnes had intentionally given her husband a fatal allergic reaction, citing money as the motive.

WIFE DENIES CAUSING DEADLY ALLERGIC REACTION had been Wanda's reaction to Janvier's theory.

Then, there was **SECRET LOVER CONFESSES TO KILLING RIVAL**.

Leon had switched the red plastic cups so that Eric would drink a real Palmito made with pineapple. But, had Leon's switcheroo killed Eric?

Scratching his chin, Beanie reflected on Wanda's theory that Michelle Ward, Eric's ex-wife had poisoned him. Again, Wanda had plausible points to make Beanie think. Eric and Michelle were bitterly opposed regarding her custody battle. Eric had told Beanie he planned to make sure Michelle lost custody of her children. As Caleb had said, it was risky to threaten a mother with the loss of her kids. Michelle had motive. But what about means?

If Wanda was right, and Eric had been poisoned, then Michelle could have done it, considering her access to pharmaceutical drugs and chemical compounds. Of course, Beanie couldn't forget Ted's bombshell—Michelle had shot and killed her second husband. As for opportunity, Beanie didn't know. Michelle had shown up uninvited to the Thanksgiving party, but Eric had slammed the door in her face. Was it possible she'd somehow snuck into the backyard and mingled, unnoticed, amongst the guests, biding her time, waiting for the opportunity to spike Eric's drink?

Beanie shook his head. He really couldn't see that happening, but he supposed anything was possible.

"Hey, you want to get some lunch?"

Glancing up, Beanie grinned at Stevie, dressed like a slacker surfer in board shorts and a T-shirt, which probably cost more than Beanie made in a month.

"Sounds good," said Beanie. "First though, I need your help."

"With what?" asked Stevie, dropping down in the chair in front of Beanie's small desk.

"Is your cousin back from Africa?" asked Beanie, hopeful.

Stevie shook his head. "But I could probably get a message to my cousin. When you asked for help a few days ago, I hadn't heard from my cousin."

"But he's since called you?"

Frowning, Stevie asked, "Why do you always think my cousin is a guy?"

"Yeah, I don't know. Because I don't know if your cousin is a man or a woman," said Beanie. "Because you won't tell us and you won't introduce us to your cousin."

"My cousin needs to remain anonymous, for obvious reasons."

"Right. Of course." Beanie cleared his throat. "Anyway, I'm hoping your cousin can help with the Eric Barnes case. I have his cell phone, but it's password protected. Think your cousin can unlock it?"

Stevie laughed. "Hasn't my cousin always been able to unlock a phone?"

Beanie chuckled. Stevie had a point. Whenever there was a password to be discovered, Stevie's hacker cousin never disappointed.

"What's on the cell phone you need to see?"

"Wanda Barnes claims there are threatening texts sent to Eric from his ex-wife, Michelle Ward," said Beanie. "Wanda thinks that will prove that Michelle poisoned him."

"What do you think?" asked Stevie.

"Michelle does have a motive," said Beanie. "Eric was going to testify against her."

"And she worked at Vaughn Pharma. Had access to drugs," said Stevie. "And she killed her second husband."

"But I don't think she would have had a chance to poison Eric at the party," said Beanie. "Not without being seen. And I can't discount Leon's confession. I think it was a terrible accident. Unless maybe … "

"Maybe what?" prompted Stevie.

Beanie finished his coffee, then said, "What if Eric's drink wasn't spiked? What if he was poisoned some other way?"

18

"Why am I not surprised that Wanda thinks I killed Eric?"

Beanie regarded Michelle Ward, Eric's ex-wife, as she shoved a hand into the wide front pocket of her white lab coat. Pulling out a pack of cigarettes and a lighter, she sat again.

Two days had passed since Beanie called Michelle and she agreed to see him. He'd secured the interview without Stevie's help, which somehow made him feel better.

They met in the small outdoor park behind the Vaughn Pharma building, where a wide pedestrian path meandered in an oblong loop around a manmade pond. Several employees strode along the pebbly gravel. Some walked leisurely. Others, in workout clothes, jogged. It was a breezy, overcast day. At two in the afternoon, the sun had yet to make an appearance, but Beanie didn't mind. With elevated humidity, harsh, bright rays would have rendered the day unbearable.

"She's such a nagging fishwife." Michelle pulled a cigarette from the pack and lit it. "I have no idea what Eric saw in that sea hag."

Beanie suspected Eric had been attracted to Wanda's physical endowments but figured Michelle wouldn't appreciate his opinion.

"I didn't kill Eric, by the way." Michelle sucked on the cigarette, her cheeks hollowing, then blew a long stream of smoke away from Beanie. "Just so you know. Put that in your article. I categorically deny each and every one of Wanda's ridiculous accusations. She's such a cow."

Beanie cleared his throat. "Well, who do you think killed Eric?"

Michelle took another sucking drag on the cigarette, then allowed the smoke to stream from her nose. "Well, I don't think Wanda did it, despite her accusations toward me."

Beanie was surprised. He'd assumed the ex-wife would finger the widow.

"She doesn't have the sense God gave a goat to successfully murder someone," said Michelle, staring at the tip of the burning cigarette.

Staring at a Vaughn Pharma employee power walking down the path, Beanie said, "What about Leon?"

Blowing another column of smoke from her mouth, Michelle said, "I believe him. He says he switched the plastic cups. I can see that happening."

"So you think Eric's death could have been a horrible mistake?"

"Possibly," said Michelle, nodding her head.

Beanie said, "Wanda doesn't think Eric died of an allergic reaction. She says he would have broken out in hives and experienced shortness of breath. She believes he was poisoned."

Michelle snorted her derision. "How would she know? Since when did she become a doctor? My money is on the secret lover—Leon."

Michelle finished her cigarette, dropped it on the ground, then smashed it with the skinny heel of her right shoe. "You should talk to Eric's friends Keith, and Aaron. They've known Eric longer than I have. They might have some idea of who could have killed him. Anyway, I should get back."

Clearing his throat, Beanie said, "Before you go ... listen, I didn't want to bring this up, but I need to find out if it's true."

"If what's true?"

"I was told that you killed your second husband."

"It was self-defense!" Michelle said. "He was a deranged stalker who came after me. He broke into my home and attacked me. So, what do you think? I killed one husband, so it was no problem for me to kill another?"

Wary of Michelle's increasing anger, Beanie said, "I'm just trying to find out the truth."

"The truth, Mr. Bean, is that I did not kill Eric," insisted Michelle.

"Even though he was going to testify against you in your child custody hearing?" asked Beanie. "Even though he was going to make sure you lost your children?"

Michelle's face went crimson. "I couldn't have killed Eric. I wasn't even at the party."

"We both know that's not true," said Beanie. "You showed up uninvited."

"Eric told you that?"

"I was in the house when you rang the doorbell," said Beanie. "I heard you arguing with him. You had motive. And probably means, too."

"Means?" Michelle frowned. "How could I have killed Eric?"

"Wanda thinks that with your access to drugs," began Beanie, "you could have given Eric something, some type of drug that would kill him but wouldn't show up in an autopsy or on a toxicology report."

"Do I look like I care what that dingbat thinks?" Michelle ranted. "Listen, the only thing I've ever given Eric was a few fentanyl patches, because he had a back problem. I regret doing it because he was becoming addicted."

"Eric said you were the one with the addiction," said Beanie. "That's why he was going to testify against you. Because you were under the influence when— "

"I had a problem managing a situation with prescription medication," said Michelle, glaring at him. "But I was not addicted."

Rising to his feet, Beanie said, "Listen—"

"No, you listen," said Michelle. "I didn't kill Eric, but if that's what you think ... prove it ..."

And with that, Eric's ex-wife pivoted and walked away.

19

"I can understand why Wanda believes Michelle killed Eric," said Eric's friend Aaron Mamet.

Aaron lived on a quiet, picturesque cul-de-sac in Allegra Shores, a companion neighborhood of Adagio Bay. The development of affluent homes was built for those who were wealthy but not prosperous enough to buy into Avalon Estates. Aaron's home, a large pale lavender bungalow, featured tropical landscaping and palm trees flanking the steps leading up to the veranda.

A day after his conversation with Michelle Ward, Beanie took the woman's advice and contacted Eric's friend Aaron.

Sitting in the spacious, sunny living room, with its peach and aqua color scheme, Beanie asked, "You think Michelle gave Eric a dose of something lethal?"

"She does have access to all sorts of drugs," said Aaron. "But, more than anything, Michelle hates Eric. And she killed her second husband. Did you know that?"

Nodding, Beanie said, "Michelle told me it was self-defense."

"That's what she claims, but I'm not so sure about that," said Aaron.

"She didn't have to kill the man. She'd hired Eric to protect her from the guy. He used to work at a security firm."

"She didn't mention hiring Eric."

"That's how she and Eric met," said Aaron. "She gave him a story about her husband stalking her. I'm not sure that was true."

"If Eric was supposed to be protecting Michelle, how did she end up killing her husband?" asked Beanie. "She told me her husband broke into her home. Shouldn't Eric have prevented that?"

"He was out of town on another assignment," said Aaron. "But, to be honest …"

Waiting, Beanie scratched his chin.

After a reflective sigh, Aaron said, "Actually, I don't think Michelle killed Eric."

"But Eric was planning to testify against her."

"Nevertheless," said Aaron, "I still don't think Michelle killed him."

"Even though you don't believe she killed her second husband in self-defense?"

"You want to know who I think killed Eric?" Aaron leaned forward, his eyes intense. "Wanda."

Beanie said, "Eric's friend Ted said the same thing. Eric's death was a horrible mistake."

"I don't think it was a mistake."

Intrigued, Beanie asked, "You don't?"

"This story about that guy Leon switching the plastic cups is ridiculous," said Aaron. "Wanda convinced him to do that."

"You think so?"

Aaron scoffed. "Wanda can be a very convincing woman when she needs to be. That guy Leon is a simp. Blinded by Wanda's lies. Wanda's telling anyone who will listen that Eric was poisoned. She should know since she poisoned him."

"You think Wanda put something in Eric's drink?"

"And it wasn't pineapple juice," said Aaron.

"Why do you think Wanda killed Eric?"

"Around February of last year," began Aaron, "Eric came into a considerable sum of money. Don't ask me where the money came from because I don't know. What I do know is that it was enough for Eric to pay cash for the house in Oyster Farms."

"Interesting," said Beanie. "So you think what?"

"I think Eric had some money left over," said Aaron. "And Wanda wanted it, so she killed him. And, of course, she also wanted the insurance death benefit money. As soon as she can collect on the claim, she's going to take that cash and disappear."

"You sound pretty sure about that," remarked Beanie.

"I'm sure because that seems to be Wanda's M.O."

"Her M.O.?"

Aaron said, "Wanda's first husband died under mysterious circumstances, and she received a very substantial insurance settlement."

20

Driving from Aaron Mamet's house in Allegra Shores, Beanie used the Bluetooth function on his cell phone to call Wanda Barnes.

"I hope I'm not disturbing you," said Beanie, after he and Wanda exchanged quick pleasantries.

"Well, I can't say I'm not disturbed," said Wanda. "But, you're not disturbing me. It's just everything going on with Eric's death and me being accused of murder and ... anyway, I don't mean to ramble. You called for a reason. Is it about what happened to Eric? Have there been any new developments in the case?"

"Not that I know of," said Beanie, navigating a traffic circle as he drove toward the center of town. "The reason I'm calling is because I spoke with Eric's friend, Aaron. I wanted to get a statement from him about Eric's passing."

"And what did he have to say?" asked Wanda. "Wait. Let me guess. He thinks I killed Eric for the insurance money, doesn't he?"

Slightly shocked, Beanie said, "Well ... yes."

"He already shared his opinion with me," said Wanda. "He seems to think that because I received an insurance settlement after my first husband died that I killed Eric."

"He spoke about mysterious circumstances surrounding your first husband's death," said Beanie, wondering if Wanda would speak about it.

"There's nothing mysterious about a heart attack," said Wanda. "My first husband was significantly older than me. His children did accuse me of not calling an ambulance quickly enough, but that wasn't true. He'd passed out while I was shopping. By the time I got home, he'd been unconscious for twenty minutes, according to the doctors. There was no way to save him. Still, his kids never liked me so I wasn't surprised they blamed me."

Beanie wasn't shocked by the suspicions of the first husband's children. Whenever an older man—known to have a much younger wife—keeled over, there was always the thought that the death might not have been natural.

Clearing his throat, Beanie said, "Aaron is also suspicious about some money Eric came into last year, and—"

"He thinks I killed Eric for that money, too?" Wanda scoffed.

"He did seem concerned that—"

"Aaron is a world-class—"

"I know it's none of my business," began Beanie, making a left turn onto the main boulevard leading into downtown St. Killian. "But … where did Eric get the money?"

"You're right, it is none of your business," Wanda said. "But, if you must know, Eric got the money from Ted."

***

"Thanks for agreeing to see me on such short notice," said Beanie, walking into the foyer of Ted Collins' Adagio Bay condo.

After his conversation with Wanda, Beanie decided to call Ted and request a follow-up interview.

"So how is the investigation into Eric's death going?" asked Ted, closing the front door. "Any new leads? Or, do the police still think

Wanda killed Eric?"

"Do you still think she didn't?" Asked Beanie as Ted led him into the living room.

Ted's gaze was shrewd. "You sound like you think I shouldn't believe she's innocent?"

"Aaron told me that Ted came into some money, which he used to buy the Oyster Farms house," said Beanie, taking a seat in a chair adjacent to the couch. "And Wanda told me you gave Eric the money."

"Well, I've been fortunate in my business dealings," said Ted, dropping down onto the couch. "And Eric was a dear friend. Little Turkey was no place for him to build a life. I just wanted him to have a chance to thrive. I was happy to help."

"That was very generous of you," said Beanie.

Ted gave a small smile. "So, let me guess. Aaron thinks Wanda killed Eric?"

"He thinks she wanted the insurance settlement and the money left over from the gift you gave Eric," said Beanie.

Shaking his head, Ted said, "Sometimes, I don't know about Aaron. Why is he so eager to pin Eric's death on Wanda?"

"Not sure about that," said Beanie. "But—"

"I'm going to leave now Mr. Collins ..."

Startled, Beanie glanced over his shoulder.

Shuffling into the living room was a heavy-set island woman wearing a plain gray housekeeper's uniform. "I'm all finished up, Mr. Collins, so if you don't need anything else."

"That's fine, Effie," said Ted, standing. As he walked the maid to the door, he said, "But, remember, call me Mr. Clark."

Laughing, the maid said, "Oh, that's right, Mr. Clark. I keep forgetting."

Moments later, when Effie was gone and Ted had returned to the couch, Beanie said, "For a moment, I thought I'd forgotten your last name."

Shrugging, Ted said, "Clark-Collins is my official last name, but the family has always gone by Clark. Effie cleaned house for my grandfather, who preferred to go by Collins. Anyway, as we were saying…"

Recalling the conversation thread, Beanie said, "I wonder if maybe someone else knew about the money you gave Eric?"

Ted frowned. "I don't think anyone other than Eric and Wanda knew, but—"

"You don't know for sure?"

"I suppose it's possible that Eric told someone," said Ted. "Can't imagine who. Or, why Eric would do that."

"Well, if he did," said Beanie. "I wonder if that person killed him."

"You mean, maybe that person wanted money, and Eric refused to fork over the cash?" Ted leaned back.

"You think it's possible?" asked Beanie.

Exhaling, Ted said, "Anything is possible. The real question is … is it probable."

21

"Just because Wanda collected insurance money from her first husband's death doesn't mean she killed Eric," said Sophie. "I mean, it's interesting, but it's not proof."

Beanie leaned back in the plastic chair where he sat at a table in the *Palmchat Gazette* breakroom. An hour ago, he'd returned to the office after spending most of the morning and midafternoon covering a high-speed police chase in Little Turkey.

Back at his tiny desk in his small cubicle, Beanie crafted the story. But, in the back of his mind, he ruminated on Eric Barnes' case. Once the Little Turkey police chase story was written and sent to Vivian for review, he'd wasted no time engaging his coworkers, Caleb, Sophie, and Stevie, in a speculation session.

"But it shows a propensity," said Caleb. "And the truth is that criminals tend to stick to the same crimes that they pulled off successfully."

"And Wanda and Leon were discussing killing Eric," reminded Stevie.

Beanie took a sip of coffee. "Leon insists that Wanda wanted nothing to do with killing Eric, but from the conversation I overheard, she seemed to be willing to consider it."

"I'll bet Wanda was gaslighting Leon."

"Gaslighting Leon how?" demanded Sophie. "The man confessed to switching the plastic cups and he didn't mention that Wanda told him to do it."

"Because Wanda didn't tell him to do it," said Caleb. "Not directly. But she could have indirectly manipulated him with subtle clues. Leon might have believed that Wanda did want to kill Eric but that she didn't want to admit it out of some misguided loyalty."

"If that's true, then that's on Leon," said Sophie, taking a swig of her orange juice. "That's why people shouldn't assume. That's why people should take people at their word."

Stevie said, "Well, Leon confessed, so …"

Nodding, Beanie said, "Yeah, he did, and I believe him, but … "

"But what?" asked Caleb.

"What if Eric didn't die from an allergic reaction?" asked Beanie. "I'm hoping the M.E. does the autopsy soon. Right now, the cause of death is pending."

"You think he was poisoned?" asked Sophie.

"It's possible," said Beanie.

"By his ex-wife?" asked Stevie.

"Maybe. Maybe not," said Beanie. "Although Michelle works at Vaughn Pharma and has access to drugs. She might have given Eric something."

"At the party?" asked Stevie.

Beanie said, "Most likely."

"But how?" Stevie asked. "I mean, she didn't stay at the party."

"She talked to Eric at the door for about ten, maybe fifteen minutes," said Beanie.

Sophie said, "What if she gave him some sort of time-released drug?"

Frowning, Stevie said, "A time-released drug?"

"Something she gave him days ago," said Sophie, her eyes flashing with excitement. "But it took a few days to work through his system and kill him."

Shaking his head, Stevie said, "I don't know about that …"

Beanie said, "Actually doesn't seem that farfetched."

Caleb said, "The ex-wife might have access to a drug like that."

"That would give her means," said Sophie. "And opportunity."

"She's got motive," said Stevie. "She didn't want Eric to testify against her."

Nodding, Beanie said, "If Michelle poisoned Eric before the party, then she could have been sitting with him at a coffee shop and put a few drops of something in his latte when he wasn't looking."

Stevie asked, "Why would Eric and Michelle have coffee together if they hated each other?"

"I don't know that they had coffee together," said Beanie, annoyed by Stevie's literalness. "All I was trying to say was that Michelle obviously saw him before the Thanksgiving party. They argued about him testifying against her, and …"

"And what?" asked Sophie.

"She might have offered him another patch," said Beanie, recalling the conversation he'd overheard between Michelle and Eric.

"What?" asked Caleb.

Stevie asked, "What do you mean?"

"What kind of patch?" demanded Sophie.

"Remember I told you the receptionist at Vaughn Pharma said there was a rumor that Michelle was stealing fentanyl patches?" asked Beanie. "Well, when Michelle and Eric were arguing at the Thanksgiving party, she offered him a patch, which sounded almost like a bribe, but he said he didn't want it."

"You think she poisoned him with a fentanyl patch?" asked Caleb.

"Not necessarily fentanyl, but …" Beanie sighed. "I just

remembered their conversation and I'm wondering if Michelle might have offered him a patch *before* the Thanksgiving party. A patch he accepted. A patch that killed him."

22

"Janvier doesn't like any other suspects besides Wanda Barnes," said Officer Damon Fields.

Taking a sip of coffee, purchased moments ago at the Hullabaloo Coffee cart in Pourciau Square, Beanie felt a jolt of excitement that had nothing to do with the caffeine.

An hour ago, he'd called Fields to get an update on the Eric Barnes case. Fields had suggested they meet for a quick afternoon java break. Under a darkening sky with heavy charcoal clouds, they sat at a wooden bistro table in the Queen Palm park, a large grassy quad designated for outdoor eating.

"What's his take on Leon's confession?"

"The way Janvier sees it, Leon is a lovesick idiot taking the blame for a woman who plans to collect a fat insurance check and leave him in the dust."

"Hate to admit this," said Beanie. "But Janvier could be right."

Chuckling, Fields stood. "And yet something tells me he's not."

Moments later, after Fields walked away, heading back to the station, Beanie scratched his jaw and took another sip of coffee. Janvier could be right about Wanda and Leon plotting to kill Eric.

Still, he didn't think he could rule out Michelle Ward as a suspect. The pharmaceutical researcher definitely could have poisoned Eric. If, in fact, the man had been poisoned. As far as he knew, the Medical Examiner still hadn't performed an autopsy on Eric. Suppose he determined that Eric had suffered a fatal allergic reaction? If that happened, Beanie would have to wonder if maybe Caleb was right and Wanda had manipulated Leon into switching the plastic cups.

Beanie's cell phone rang, interrupting his musing.

As the faint rumble of thunder cut through the gusty, rain-scented breeze, Beanie answered. "Roland Bean."

"Mr. Bean? My name is Keith Cox," said a gravely, unfamiliar male voice.

Curious, Beanie said, "Yes?"

"I'm a friend of Eric Barnes," the man said. "You and I met at the Thanksgiving party."

"Right," said Beanie, recalling the man. "How are you?"

"Fine, fine," said Cox. "Listen, I don't want to take up too much of your time."

"No, it's okay," said Beanie. "How can I help you?"

"Ted and Aaron told me you spoke to them about Eric's case," said Cox. "I was hoping you would call me but you didn't so I decided to call you."

"I did have you on my list to call," said Beanie, mentally kicking himself. "I wanted to get your thoughts about the case."

"I have an idea who might have killed him," said Cox. "I just don't have a name."

Beanie frowned. "You don't have a name?"

"It's the person who sent Eric those emails," said Cox. "But I don't know who that person is …"

Thunder rumbled. "Emails?" Beanie echoed.

"Someone was sending Eric crazy emails," Cox said. "The subject lines were weird and there was no message in the body of the email."

Remembering his promise to look into the emails Eric had shown him, Beanie said, "Eric told you about those emails?"

"He told you?"

"He asked me to look into them," said Beanie. "I promised I would, but then he died, and …"

"Eric was worried about those emails," said Cox. "He thought they might be related to something from Wanda's past."

"From Wanda's past?"

Cox said, "Wanda's first husband died under strange circumstances, and she got a huge insurance settlement."

Beanie nodded. "Aaron Mamet told me about that."

"Well, I don't think Aaron knew that Wanda's first husband's kids believed she'd killed their father," said Keith.

"Wanda told me about that," said Beanie.

"Did Wanda tell you the first husband's daughter threatened her? Apparently told Wanda that she would kill someone that Wanda loved … meaning Eric. The daughter told Wanda it would be an eye for an eye situation. This was when Wanda and Eric still lived in California. That's actually why they moved back to the island. Eric thought maybe Wanda's ex-stepdaughter was sending the emails."

"But if I recall, the emails seemed to suggest that the person wanted Eric to tell the truth about something," said Beanie. "There was no mention of Wanda."

"Look, maybe it wasn't the first husband's daughter. All I know is if you can find out who sent those emails," said Cox, "you might find out who killed Eric."

23

At home, after picking up Ethan and Evan from Noelle's mom's house in Handweg, Beanie fixed the little tykes a snack—apples, peanut butter, and chocolate milk—and decided not to protest when they begged to watch television.

Normally, Beanie would have taken them into the backyard to run around and burn off excess energy, but he was eager to examine the mysterious emails. He'd been anxious since his conversation with Keith earlier that afternoon. Returning to the paper to work on his follow-up piece about the Little Turkey police chase had been a chore. Fingers on the keyboard, he'd managed to craft the story, but his attention wavered, wandering back to the emails.

Initially, Beanie had wondered if the emails were somehow connected to Eric's death. When Stevie's hacker cousin had been unavailable to trace the email address, Beanie had put the theory on the back burner. But he was eager to revisit the idea that Eric's killer might have sent the man the strange emails.

Now, sitting at the desk in the small study he shared with Noelle, Beanie retrieved the emails from the INBOX tray where he'd stashed them.

With an exhale, he took a breath and read the emails.

From: coolkidstable@palmmail.net
To: ebarnes@palmmail.net
Date: October 5
Re: I need answers

From: coolkidstable@palmmail.net
To: ebarnes@palmmail.net
Date: October 9
Re: I need to know what happened

From: coolkidstable@palmmail.net
To: ebarnes@palmmail.net
Date: October 14
Re: We should talk

From: coolkidstable@palmmail.net
To: ebarnes@palmmail.net
Date: October 16
Re: Tell me the truth

Beanie sighed. Rubbed his eyes. He re-read the emails again. *I need answers. I need to know what happened.* Obviously, the person behind the coolkidstable email address believed Eric could provide the answers. But about what? Beanie focused on the word "need." It suggested an urgency. Maybe desperation. A need was something essential. Something critical for survival. Shuffling through the emails again,

Beanie scanned the subject lines. An idea came to him. He wondered what might happen if he sent a response email.

"Daddy! Daddy! Daddy!"

The high-pitched whooping and yelling reached Beanie before Ethan came barreling into the study, arms windmilling as he spun around like a whirling dervish.

"What are you doing, Daddy?" demanded Ethan, hopping around the study.

Putting the emails away before Ethan grabbed them, Beanie said, "Daddy was just looking at some documents for work."

"What kind of documents?" asked Ethan, skipping in a circle.

"Just something for a story Daddy is working on," said Beanie.

Seconds later, little Evan toddled into the room, laughing, and clapping his hands. "Daddy! Daddy!"

"Hey, Bud," said Beanie, bending over to scoop Evan into his arms and onto his lap.

"I want to see the documents, Daddy," said Ethan, his face an expression of earnest interest.

"I already put them away," said Beanie. "Why don't we go outside before Mommy comes home?"

"But I want to see the documents," said Ethan, his tone hinting at a major tantrum if he didn't get his way.

"Documents!" echoed Evan. "Want to see documents!"

"Are the documents a secret, Daddy?" asked Ethan, a mischievous gleam in his eye.

Beanie considered the question. "More like a mystery."

"A mystery!" Ethan jumped up and down. "Like the Hardy Boys, Daddy?"

"Yeah, sort of like the Hardy Boys," said Beanie.

"Hardy Boy!" Evan giggled. "Hardy Boy!"

Recently, Ethan had found an old Hardy Boys mystery novel in the book swap box at the library. The books were above his reading level but Ethan had been drawn to the cover, with its hand-drawn adventure scene of Frank and Joe running from a speeding car. Beanie had been reading a chapter to Ethan and Evan every night for the past two weeks.

"Can I solve the mystery, Daddy?" begged Ethan. "Please! Please!"

"Solve the mystery!" said Evan, squirming on Beanie's lap, a clear signal that he wanted to be allowed to roam free around the study. "Solve the mystery!"

"I can figure out who the bad guys are, Daddy!" promised Ethan. "We can put them in jail where they belong!"

Chuckling, Beanie ruffled the short curls of Ethan's fauxhawk. "Let's go out in the backyard, okay? We can come up with a plan to catch the bad guys."

"What about the documents?"

Beanie wasn't surprised by the question. Ethan could be like a dog with a bone sometimes.

"We'll look at them later," said Beanie, securing his hold on Evan as he stood and took Ethan's hand.

"Okay, Daddy," said Ethan. "Are the documents hidden in a secret place? We don't want the bad guys to find them."

"They won't," said Beanie, heading out of the study.

"Are you sure, Daddy?" asked Ethan, undisguised skepticism in his tone. "We need those documents to solve the mystery!"

"You know what, Buddy?" Beanie reflected on his idea to send a response to the coolkidstable email. "I think you might be right."

24

The next morning, sitting at the desk in his small cubicle at the *Palmchat Gazette* offices, Beanie crafted an email to send to the coolkidstable email. He'd meant to send the message the night before, but after roughhousing and horse playing with his boys in the backyard for several hours, Beanie had been too exhausted to think about work.

After finishing his first cup of coffee of the morning, Beanie fact-checked a few articles, sent them to Vivian for review, and then focused on the coolkidstable email. With Keith's suggestion in his head—if you can find out who sent those emails, you might find out who killed Eric—Beanie was eager to know if he could get coolkidstable to respond.

Beanie wasn't exactly sure what to write, but he figured keeping things simple, and somewhat vague, might work. Fingers on the keys, he wrote …

If you need the truth, I might be able to help you find the answers.

Respond to this email if you'd like to talk.

With a sigh, Beanie leaned back. Hand on the mouse, he hovered the cursor over the SEND button. Had he written a compelling message? One that would interest and entice? And spur coolkidstable into contacting him? He wasn't sure. And he wouldn't know unless he sent the message.

Rereading what he'd written, Beanie felt a pang of indecisiveness. Should he write something different? Something more? Should he introduce himself? Explain who he was and how he knew Eric?

His desk phone buzzed. The Caller-ID showed an interoffice call. His boss, Vivian.

Moving his hand from the mouse, he grabbed the receiver and answered. "Hey, what's up?"

"Someone tried to rob a bank in Little Turkey," said Vivian.

"What?"

"I need you to get down there now," said Vivian. "And I'll need the first draft before the end of the day."

"No problem," said Beanie, replacing the receiver on the base.

Glancing at the computer, Beanie grabbed the mouse and clicked the SEND button before he changed his mind.

Thirty minutes later, at the crime scene, Beanie got the details from two first responders.

As he walked back to his car, Beanie's phone beeped, signaling an email. Slowing his stride, he accessed his email account. Beanie's heart started to thud as he stared at the message.

From: coolkidstable@palmmail.net

To: roland.bean@palmchatgazette.net

Re: please contact me

Hey, not sure what answers you are talking about but very curious!! Love your stories!!! We can meet at Adagio Bay mall at Cup-O-Joe where I work. How about 4 p.m.? My shift is at 5. Let me know!!!! Hope to see you soon!!! PS – my name is Ash!!

Disappointment coursed through Beanie as he pointed the key fob toward the vehicle and opened the door to his SUV remotely. Inside the car, he re-read the email. Obviously, it wasn't from the person who'd emailed Eric Barnes. The responder wasn't looking for answers. But whoever had responded was curious. And liked his articles, thought Beanie, tossing the phone onto the passenger seat as he buckled the seatbelt.

But Beanie doubted the sender—Ash had any connection to the daughter of Wanda's first husband. Ash lived in St. Killian while the first husband's daughter was in California. Beanie hadn't given much credence to Keith's theory, anyway. It was interesting information, however, and he hoped to discuss the daughter with Wanda.

Driving back to the *Palmchat Gazette*, Beanie contemplated whether or not to meet Ash at the Adagio Bay outdoor mall. Someone had sent Eric emails from the coolkidstable account. Ash hadn't sent them, but maybe she—or he—knew who had reached out to Eric.

25

Later that afternoon, around three o'clock, after finishing the final draft of his story and sending it to Vivian for review, Beanie went to the breakroom. Making himself a third cup of coffee, he reflected on the decision he'd made earlier about meeting Ash. He wasn't so sure it was a good idea anymore. What if it was a waste of time? Beanie took a sip of coffee. He supposed he wouldn't know unless he headed to the mall.

An hour later, Beanie sat across from Ash, a bubbly, animated twentysomething with fresh-scrubbed cheeks, a winning smile, and a pile of loose curls piled on top of her head and secured by a large clip.

Gesturing with her hands, which sported silver rings on each finger and both thumbs, she said, "And that story you wrote about the woman found dead at the Easter egg hunt was so awesome sauce!"

"Thanks," said Beanie, trying to recall if anyone had ever called his writing awesome sauce. It was a compliment, he figured. One of the many Ash had bestowed upon him since he'd joined her at one of the bistro tables outside the Cup-O-Joe coffee shop at the Adagio Bay outdoor mall.

"If it weren't for you," said Ash, "the killer would not have been caught!"

"Well, I think the police had more to do with apprehending the killer than I did."

"And then that story about the guy found dead in the jungle!" Ash shook her head as she let out a little squeak of delight. "And he was your neighbor and his wife attacked you and then you almost got burned to death trying to uncover the murderer!"

"It was intense," said Beanie, hoping to steer the young woman to the topic of the coolkidstable emails.

"Oh, and I almost forgot to tell you this," she said. "Your intern, and his girlfriend, Friday, are my friends, too! We go to school together! How crazy is that?"

Beanie nodded. "Small world, huh?"

"Very small, indeed," agreed Ash, laughing, an infectious giggle that reminded Beanie of little Evan. He wouldn't have been surprised if the young woman started clapping her hands.

Cognizant of the time—he had to pick up the boys from his mother-in-law's house at six p.m.—Beanie glanced at his watch, and said, "So … about the email I sent you …"

"Oh, yes, of course!" Ash's eyes widened and her nostrils flared slightly, accentuating her small nose ring. "I was like, ohmigosh, what is this about? Answers that I need? What? Do I need answers about something? I had no idea what was going on! At first, I thought it was a prank, but then after I confronted my roommates, Shanna and Charlotte, and they, like, swore they hadn't sent the email, I figured I needed to find out what was going on, so I emailed you back and you wanted to meet, so—"

"So, here we are," interrupted Beanie, desperate to get a word in edgewise, which Ash seemed capable of preventing. "And I should probably explain—"

"Oh, yes, please do!" Ash exclaimed, her green eyes dancing with excitement.

"A few weeks ago," began Beanie, "emails from the address, coolkidstable, were sent to an acquaintance of mine, and he wanted to know the identity of the sender."

Eyebrows furrowed, Ash said, "I didn't send any messages from coolkidstable, but I know who did."

"You do?"

Nodding, Ash leaned back and rolled her eyes. "My old roommate, Oscar Reed. He didn't have a computer, so I let him borrow my laptop a few times. He created that email account. Coolkidstable. I was, like, what does that mean? I don't even think he knew. Anyway, I don't normally check Oscar's emails. I accidentally opened it when I was looking for an old email my aunt sent me last year. Crazy coincidence, huh?"

"Seems that way," said Beanie as something within him began to deflate. "Your old roommate?"

"I had to kick him out," said Ash.

"Why?" asked Beanie.

"He stopped paying rent," explained Ash. "Last I heard, he was back living with his mom in Seashell Estates."

"Do you have his mother's address?"

Ash shook her head. "But I have her number. I can give it to you."

"I'd appreciate that," said Beanie.

Scrolling through her phone, Ash asked, "Why was Oscar emailing your friend about needing answers?"

"That's what I hope Oscar can tell me," said Beanie.

"Okay, I emailed you Oscar's mom's number!" announced Ash. "Hopefully he can give you the answers that you need!"

"Hopefully," agreed Beanie, standing.

Ash stood as well. "Hey, it was really good to meet you!"

"And you as well," said Beanie, giving her a smile.

"Before you go," said Ash. "I want to tell you that I'm really enjoying your stories about that guy who dropped dead at the

Thanksgiving party! And the fact that you were there! How is it that you're always at the wrong place at the right time?"

Beanie chuckled. "You know, I wonder that myself sometimes."

26

"I haven't seen him in five or six months," said Heather Reed, her expression a mix of worry and disgust as she perched on the edge of the couch, hands clasped, resting between her knees. Wearing a baseball cap with a mass of hair pulled between the opening in the back, gym shorts, and an oversized T-shirt, she appeared ready for an afternoon run. After Beanie knocked on the door, introduced himself, and stated his business, Heather Reed admitted that she had, in fact, been thinking about going for a run.

"But just thinking," she'd said with a nervous laugh.

Since she hadn't yet made up her mind, she was fine with talking to him.

After his conversation with Ash yesterday, Beanie had decided to call Oscar Reed's mother as soon as he arrived at work this morning. With his first cup of coffee, he'd made his first and second calls to the number Ash had given him. Heather Reed hadn't answered, and Beanie decided not to leave a voice mail. The situation with Oscar was complicated. Not something easily articulated in thirty seconds.

As early morning segued slowly into mid-morning, the news day proved to be slow. With no breaking stories to cover, Beanie decided to take an early lunch. Instead of the Loco Goat food truck at Pourciau Square, he decided to take a chance and drop by Heather Reed's home unannounced.

Normally, he didn't like to ambush witnesses or persons of interest —it was a good way to get cursed out, or a door slammed in your face, or a warning to vacate the premises or the cops would be called. But he was anxious to find Oscar and talk to him.

Ash was convinced that Oscar had sent the messages to Eric Barnes, as the coolkidstable was an email account he'd created. But what if someone else had used the account? An email account could be accessed and used from any location in the world. Just as Ash had allowed Oscar to use her laptop, Oscar could have allowed someone to use his computer. Or, he could have emailed the messages, from the coolkidstable account, on behalf of someone else.

But, if Oscar had sent the message to Eric, then the next question was, why? How did he know Eric? What answers did he need from Eric? And had his demand for answers led him to kill Eric?

Following a quick reverse search of Heather Reed's phone number, Beanie located her address and left the office. Twenty minutes later, he turned into the neighborhood of Seashell Estates, which was somewhat of a misnomer as the neighborhood was not comprised of large, grand homes, but of modest shotgun houses on small lots.

Well-manicured lawns dotted with Sago palms and fruit trees lined quiet streets that reminded Beanie of Oyster Farms, which wasn't surprising. Seashell Estates was a sister development of Oyster Farms, with the same demographics—people who made a decent living and wanted to raise their families in a safe environment.

"Why haven't you seen Oscar in such a long time?" asked Beanie.

Heather sighed. "We had a falling out. About his father."

"His father?"

Nodding, Heather said, "After Melvin—that was his dad's name— was killed, Oscar went on this single-minded quest to find out who killed his father."

"Oscar's father was murdered?"

"Shot to death." Heather took in a breath, then blew it out as she shook her head. "Oscar was devastated. Him and his dad were very close. Me and his dad was divorced but Melvin was very much an active father, even though he had moved back to St. Felipe, where he was from."

Beanie said, "So, I take it the police never found out who killed him?"

"Figured it was a robbery gone bad," said Heather. "It's funny. Melvin was a partner in an accounting firm business for a while and I always thought he'd get shot by someone who was mad because they had to pay taxes or something."

"Mad about paying taxes?" Beanie frowned. "We all have to pay taxes."

Heather chuckled softly. "Melvin would tell me that people would be upset that he couldn't work some magic and make their tax bills go away. Anyway, after the accounting firm shut down, Melvin ran a boat tour company. Had four boats and he would take people on excursions. They would go to secluded beaches. Snorkel. He made a good living doing that. His customers always gave him good reviews. In the summers, when he wasn't in school, Oscar would work the tours with his dad."

"Can you tell me a bit more about Oscar's quest to find his father's killer?"

Heather exhaled. "I'm not even really sure what all he's doing—except maybe getting himself in trouble. Last thing he told me—the reason we had the falling out—was he was thinking of suing the St. Felipe Police Department for not investigating the case properly. I told Oscar that the last thing he wanted to do was make the cops mad. He accused me of not caring who killed Melvin because we was divorced. Which wasn't true. Wasn't that I didn't care. As I tried to explain to Oscar, I believed the police. I figured they were right. Melvin got robbed. And knowing my ex-husband, he probably didn't want to give up without a fight. Anyway, Oscar stormed out and I haven't seen him since."

Beanie cleared his throat. "Mrs. Reed—"

"Heather, please," she said.

"Heather … earlier, I mentioned that I wanted to talk to Oscar because he wrote some emails to an acquaintance of mine—"

Heather shook her head. "I don't know anything about any emails Oscar wrote. Maybe it's got something to do with his search for who killed Melvin."

A fissure of excitement coursed through Beanie. "I think you might be right. Can you tell me … does Oscar know a man named Eric Barnes?"

Frowning, Heather said, "Eric Barnes? I don't know. I don't think so, but that name sounds familiar."

"Eric Barnes is the man who died after collapsing at a Thanksgiving party," explained Beanie. "I've been writing a series of articles about the case."

"That's where I know the name from," said Heather. "I've read a few of your stories. First, the cops thought the wife did it. Then they said it was the guy the wife was fooling around with. What a mess. Wait a minute … you think Oscar knew the dead guy, Eric Barnes?"

"I'm not sure," said Beanie, treading lightly as he noticed the suspicion wash across Heather's face. Last thing he wanted to do was incite her Mama Bear instincts. What he thought was that Oscar might have had something to do with Eric Barnes' death. But he couldn't let Heather know that. He couldn't get kicked out of the house before he got the information he needed.

Continuing, Beanie said, "I just want to know if Oscar did indeed send the email to Eric Barnes. And, if so, I would like to know why."

Crossing her arms over her chest, Heather asked, "What kind of emails did he send Eric Barnes? What did they say?"

Beanie hesitated. Should he be honest with Heather Reed? Tell her that Oscar wanted answers, wanted to know what happened and wanted to talk with Eric? Maybe so. As it was, his theory about Oscar killing Eric was faltering. Not making much sense anymore. No longer probable. Or maybe even possible. Learning about Oscar's quest put the emails to Eric Barnes in a different light.

Aaron Mamet believed that the person who'd sent Eric the emails had killed him.

Beanie didn't think so. If Oscar wanted Eric dead, he wouldn't have emailed him. He would have stalked Eric and killed him. If Oscar had sent the emails, as Beanie believed he had, then he wanted answers from Eric about his father's death. Oscar Reed wouldn't have killed the man who could have given him the truth.

Beanie said, "I think Oscar believed Eric Barnes knew something about his father's murder."

27

That afternoon, ruminating on his conversation with Heather Reed that morning, Beanie decided to do some investigation into Oscar Reed's father, Melvin Reed, who'd been killed in St. Felipe.

Specifically, he hoped to find a connection between Melvin Reed and Eric Barnes. Or a reason why Oscar believed that Eric Barnes might have answers about his father's death.

However, Beanie cautioned himself not to get the cart before the horse.

First of all, he still had to determine that Oscar Reed had indeed sent the emails to Eric Barnes. Ash claimed the coolkidstable email had been created by Oscar, but Heather Reed hadn't known anything about Oscar sending emails to anyone. Which didn't mean that the address didn't belong to Oscar. Considering her estrangement from her son, there were probably a lot of things Heather didn't know about Oscar.

Second of all, if Oscar had sent the emails, Beanie needed to find out why. Oscar might have wanted answers from Eric that had nothing to do with his father's death.

Still, Beanie was inclined to believe he was on the right track. He was starting to think that Oscar believed Eric knew something about the death of Melvin Reed.

Beginning with the *Palmchat Gazette* morgue, he searched to determine if the paper had covered the story of Melvin Reed's murder. Though headquartered in St. Killian, the newspaper covered stories across the entire island chain and throughout the Caribbean. There was one satellite office in St. Mateo, with its own staff, but the majority of the paper's content was generated from the St. Killian staff. Leo Bronson, the paper's owner, and publisher had plans to open more *Palmchat Gazette* locations on St. Killian's sister islands. Until that happened, the paper published stories filed by various news services, including AP, Thompson-Reuters, and Bronson Publishing, owned by Leo's father, media magnet Burt Bronson.

Beanie typed *Reed, Melvin* into the database's search engine. A minute or so later, a few article links popped up: *School children discover body behind daycare center. Daycare center murder victim identified. Police say daycare center victim feared for his life.*

After a sip of his second cup of coffee, Beanie clicked on the first article.

SCHOOL CHILDREN DISCOVER BODY BEHIND DAYCARE CENTER

AP News

St. Felipe, Palmchat Islands—Children walking on a dirt road behind a daycare center in the East Bath neighborhood on Wednesday found the body of a man who had been shot, authorities said.

St. Felipe police deputies said a group of three girls and two boys, walking home from primary school, spotted the body around 2:30 p.m. near a large trash bin.

Deputies and paramedics arrived at the scene and noted that the victim had two gunshot wounds to the back of his head.

He was pronounced dead at St. Felipe Medical Center, deputies said.

St. Felipe detectives have no suspects at this time.

Scratching his chin, Beanie printed a copy of the article. The story was pretty straightforward, as per the style and standard of the AP freelance writers. Just the facts. Details with no opinions or editorializing. Beanie thought it was horrible that kids had found the body. He shuddered to think of Noelle's reaction if Ethan, or God forbid, little Evan, stumbled upon a man shot to death.

Although, little Evan had already found a dead body.

Thank goodness, his youngest son hadn't known the dead woman had been murdered. His innocent, two-year-old mind had perceived the woman to be sleeping. That hadn't stopped Noelle from having a conniption.

Beanie read the second article, written a few days after the first.

DAYCARE CENTER MURDER VICTIM IDENTIFIED

AP News

St. Felipe, Palmchat Islands—The body of a man found shot to death behind a daycare center has been identified by authorities as Melvin Reed, 52.

Reed, a native of St. Felipe, owned a tour boat company and was known throughout his community for his charity.

A week ago, Reed's body was found by a group of children walking behind daycare on their way home from school. Reed had been shot twice in the head. Police have no suspects at the time, but Detective Elijah Freeman believes robbery may have been the motive.

"On the day the victim was killed," said Detective Freeman, "he went to the bank, where he performed several financial transactions. It's possible he was watched and then followed from the bank. The perpetrators may have believed the victim had withdrawn a large sum of money and targeted him."

Police say the investigation is still ongoing.

Beanie printed the second article then re-read it. Like the first article, it was all facts. The detective's theory was interesting. And it made sense, considering that Melvin Reed had visited the bank before he was killed. Melvin could have been targeted. Beanie understood why Heather Reed had believed the robbery motive.

But, obviously, Oscar had not.

Or, had he?

Beanie wondered if Oscar suspected Eric knew something about the robbery. But what could Oscar think that Eric knew? Thinking about the emails, Beanie recalled the subject line: *I need to know what happened*. Did Oscar think Eric knew what happened to Melvin? Beanie refined the question in his head. Did Oscar think Eric knew who had robbed and killed his father? As a sly jolt passed through him, Beanie twisted the question again. Did Oscar think Eric had robbed and killed his father?

Shaking his head, Beanie stood. He needed another cup of coffee. And he needed to nix the rampant speculation.

He didn't have enough facts.

28

After making his third cup of coffee, Beanie returned to his small desk and read the last article about Melvin Reed.

POLICE SAY DAYCARE CENTER VICTIM FEARED FOR HIS LIFE.

AP News

St. Felipe, Palmchat Islands—Melvin Reed, found shot to death behind a daycare center by school children, may have feared for his life, according to police.

Reed, a tour boat operator, was found dead a week ago.

Initially, police believed robbery to be the motive for the killing, as Reed had visited a local bank before he was killed. However, Detective Elijah Freeman revealed that Reed had contacted police a month prior, fearing for his life.

"Mr. Reed believed that someone was following him and trying to kill him," said Freeman. "He spoke with police who investigated his concerns, however, we were not able to confirm his suspicions."

As to why Reed believed someone wanted to kill him, Freeman declined to speculate. The detective maintained, however, that police believe robbery was the motive behind Reed's murder.

Family members and friends reiterated that Reed was a kind man with a big heart who did not have any enemies.

"He was a good egg," said Andy Rios, who worked at the marina where Reed's boats were docked. "Always had a kind word for everybody and didn't know a stranger. Can't imagine why somebody wanted to hurt him."

Beanie printed the last article, then grabbed a pen and a pad to jot down a few notes.

His thoughts racing, he wrote: Why did Melvin Reed think someone wanted to kill him? Was that true? If so, who wanted to kill Melvin Reed? Why? Did Oscar think that Eric knew who wanted Melvin dead?

Pen hovering over the pad, Beanie hesitated to write the next question whirling through his mind. Because it was pure speculation. Conjecture. And the question wasn't based on a logical conclusion.

Still, he wrote: Did Oscar think Eric Barnes killed his father?

Beanie sat back. He should probably scratch through the last question. Why would Oscar think Eric had killed his father? Sure, Oscar wanted answers. The truth. He wanted to know what happened. But that didn't mean Oscar thought Eric was a killer. Because if he did, why not take his suspicions to the police? Or why not confront Eric outright? And yet, there had been no emails with Oscar accusing Eric of killing his father.

The idea that Oscar thought Eric was a killer was riveting, but it was an overreach. There was no proof. No thread leading back to that conclusion. No dots to connect Beanie's ideas.

And yet …

Beanie sat forward. Maybe it wasn't so inconceivable that Eric could have killed Melvin Reed.

After all—

Beanie's desk phone buzzed.

Cursing the interruption, he nevertheless lifted the receiver. It was his boss, after all. He couldn't ignore Vivian.

"Hey, what's up?"

"I just got a call from my contact in the Medical Examiner's office," said Vivian. "Eric Barnes didn't die from a fatal allergic reaction."

His heart starting to race, Beanie turned to his computer and opened a Word file. "How did he die?"

"The M.E. finally got around to doing that autopsy," said Vivian. "Eric Barnes died from a drug overdose."

29

"A drug overdose …" said Noelle, voice lowered as she put a third batch of cupcakes in the oven. Discussing death and mayhem while making treats for Evan's preschool class, which Noelle's mom would deliver the following day during show-and-tell, was not exactly ideal, Beanie figured. But he'd been anxious to talk to his wife about the details of Eric's demise.

The story he'd written—**DRUGS, NOT A PALMITO, KILLED MAN**—was trending on the *Palmchat Gazette* website and had already garnered hundreds of comments.

"A drug overdose," repeated Beanie, feeling a bit like little Evan, who was always echoing everything he heard. He was sure his wife had used a sotto voce so their youngest tyke wouldn't start chanting "Overdose! Overdose!" while giggling and clapping.

"So Eric was a drug addict?" Noelle closed the oven then grabbed the tray of cupcakes she'd allowed to cool and took it to the table. There, Ethan and Evan were putting way too many sprinkles on the first batch of cupcakes, which had already cooled and been frosted with chocolate icing.

"Apparently," said Beanie, taking a seat next to Noelle. He grabbed a cupcake, picked up a butter knife, and dipped it in the plastic container of chocolate icing.

Noelle used the second butter knife to frost the cupcake she'd picked up. "Why am I not surprised?"

Beanie frowned. "I don't know. Why aren't you surprised? I'm kind of shocked. Didn't expect the guy to be a drug addict."

"I'm not surprised because Eric Barnes lived in that house."

Beanie dug into the container of icing again. "What does that mean?"

"Roland, not too much icing, okay?" admonished Noelle, her tone only slightly exasperated.

Beanie looked at the cupcake he was working on. "How much is too much?"

"That's too much," said Noelle, pointing the knife at the cupcake Beanie held. "You only need to go over the top with icing once."

"Well, I went over it twice because there wasn't enough icing."

"That's okay," said Noelle, finishing her fourth cupcake with brisk efficiency. "Too much sugar will have the kids bouncing off the walls, and—"

"Look, Mommy! Look Mommy!" shouted Ethan, proudly presenting a cupcake doused with sprinkles. "My cupcake have the most sprinkles!"

Beanie glanced at the cupcake, which looked as though Ethan had shaken the entire plastic jar of candy sprinkles on top. Contrastingly, Evan's cupcake had three single candy sprinkles. Maybe four.

"I want spinkles, Daddy!" cried little Evan, his lower lip quivering. "Ethan have all the spinkles."

"Ethan …" Noelle sighed. "Why did you put all of the sprinkles on one cupcake?"

"Spinkles, Mommy!" complained Evan, his face scrunched in a grumpy frown. "Please, Mommy, spinkles!"

"Because I wanted the cupcake to look pretty, Mommy!"

"Bud, all the cupcakes need to look pretty," said Beanie, trying to cut the tension in the kitchen. He could tell his wife was struggling, *thisclose* to blowing a gasket.

"But this is the best cupcake, Daddy," insisted Ethan. "It tastes the yummiest!"

"Yummiest!" laughed Evan, who appeared to have forgotten to be upset about the lack of sprinkles on his cupcake. "Yummiest!"

"Bud, I'm sure all the cupcakes are yummy," said Beanie.

"No, Daddy, this one is the yummiest," said Ethan. "I can prove it!"

Curious, Beanie asked, "How?"

"I will taste it, Daddy!" announced Ethan. "And I can tell you how yummy it is!"

Noelle said, "Ethan, do not take a bite of that cupcake!"

"Why not, Mommy?" asked Ethan, as though he was confused.

"Ethan, what did I tell you?" Noelle frowned at the four-year-old. "Do not eat that cupcake."

"But, Mommy, if I don't taste the cupcake, I won't be able to prove to Daddy that it is the yummiest!"

Beanie shook his head. He had to hand it to the kid. Ethan was a little master manipulator. But he wasn't going to chuckle in appreciation of his son's slyness. At least, not in front of his wife. It was, however, a story his coworkers would appreciate over coffee in the breakroom tomorrow morning.

30

"After the Medical Examiner performed the autopsy, he found an unknown drug in Eric's bloodstream. At first, he thought it was some synthetic street drug, but subsequent tests revealed it to be a compound currently in development at Vaughn Pharma."

"A compound in development?" Beanie frowned.

Fields said, "A new pain medication the company is working on. It's not on the market yet. Hasn't even gone through any drug trials."

"How did an experimental drug end up in Eric's blood?" asked Beanie.

Fields took a sip of his iced coffee, then said, "That's what Janvier is working overtime to figure out. The crime scene techs found the Vaughn Pharma pain drug in cigarettes that were shoved in the pockets of Eric Barnes' shorts."

"Cigarettes?" echoed Beanie, recalling the cigarette Eric had talked about smoking when they'd spoken in the kitchen on the day of the Thanksgiving party. The cigarette Eric had claimed his wife didn't know he planned to smoke with his friends, Ted, Aaron, and Keith. A cigarette laced with an experimental drug that proved to be deadly.

Fields said, "The Vaughn Pharma pain drug is slightly less lethal than fentanyl, but there was still enough of it in Eric's blood to kill an elephant."

Beanie said, "Good God."

"The ME estimates the pain drug took about thirty minutes to kill Eric," said Fields.

"So, half an hour after he smoked the drug-laced cigarette, he collapsed and died."

Nodding, Fields said, "The interesting part is that not all of the cigarettes found in Barnes' shorts contained the Vaughn Pharma pain drug. Some of the cigarettes were just regular nicotine cigarettes."

Scratching his chin, Beanie sat back. "Is it possible that Eric somehow got the Vaughn Pharma pain drug himself? I know he couldn't have had a prescription for it, but he did have a connection to the company—his ex-wife Michelle. Maybe she gave him the drug. She worked in research and development. When I talked to her, she mentioned providing Eric with fentanyl patches for his back."

"So, maybe she gave him this new drug?" asked Fields. "Suppose it's possible. Question is, when did she give it to him?"

"Maybe at the Thanksgiving party," said Beanie. "She showed up. They argued, and then … well, maybe not."

Fields shook his head. "I don't think so."

A blustery breeze threatened to blow his napkin away. Beanie put his cup of coffee on top of the napkin to prevent it from flying across the quad. "What did Wanda have to say?"

Fields shook his plastic cup, rattling the ice. "She claims she knew nothing about any experimental pain medication."

"I'm sure Janvier didn't believe her," said Beanie.

Fields shook his head. "Especially not after the crime scene guys found a pack of cigarettes in Eric's office. Turns out, those cigarettes were all laced with the Vaughn Pharma drug."

Beanie was floored. "Are you serious?"

"They found Eric's prints on the cigarettes and a set of unknown male prints," said Fields. "But Wanda Barnes' prints were not found on the pack of cigarettes. Interesting thing is, there were a third set of prints on the pack of cigarettes. Unknown *female* prints."

Beanie said, "Female prints? So not Wanda's, right?

Fields shook his head. "Right."

"Wonder who they belong to?" asked Beanie.

"Janvier should be trying to find out." Fields shook his head. "But, I doubt he will. He's convinced that Wanda gave the drug-laced cigarette to Eric, so she could kill him and collect the insurance money …"

31

"I thought that when the Medical Examiner's autopsy showed that Eric didn't die of an allergic reaction, which I told the police, that Detective Janvier would catch a clue," groused Wanda Barnes, pacing across the living room of her peach bungalow.

Following his lunch with Officer Fields, Beanie returned to the *Palmchat Gazette*. After writing his story, he called Wanda and secured a face-to-face interview with Eric's widow to get her comments on the stunning developments in her dead husband's case.

"But no! Now he's come up with some cockamamie theory about me buying drug-laced cigarettes to poison Eric? That's ridiculous! First of all, I didn't even know Eric was smoking again. I am the one who convinced him to stop smoking! Why would I want him to start smoking again? And where on earth would I get cigarettes laced with drugs?"

"I agree," said Beanie. "Janvier is way off base. But that's not surprising."

Plopping down on the couch across from the chair where Beanie sat, Wanda said, "You know what I think? He wants me behind bars because I cheated on Eric, not because I killed Eric. My crime is infidelity, in Janvier's view."

Beanie didn't think that was true, but it gave him an opening to ask, "Why did you cheat on Eric? Were you having problems in the marriage?"

Wanda sighed, rubbed her eyes. "There was no good reason. I was being selfish and stupid. I got caught up because Leon was so romantic and … I regret what I did. The only good thing is I don't think Eric knew."

"What's next for you and Leon?"

"Nothing," said Wanda. "I told him I don't want to see him again. Told him I regretted the affair. He didn't take it well but said he understood. He thinks I don't want to be with him because he switched the plastic cups. The truth is, I'm not in love with Leon. I never was … I loved Eric. I miss him very much. Before he died, I was going to break things off with Leon."

Beanie was skeptical but didn't bother mentioning his doubt. No need to offend Wanda before he got the information he needed. "You have any idea where Eric got the cigarettes?"

Wanda said, "Michelle could have given Eric the drug. That makes the most sense! She works at Vaughn Pharma!"

Beanie shook his head. "I don't think so. My contacts at the police station told me that Eric died thirty minutes after he smoked the drug-laced cigarette. If Michelle had given Eric the cigarette, he would have died thirty minutes after she left the party. But that's not what happened. She left several hours *before* Eric died. Also, when Eric and I spoke in the kitchen, he had the cigarette before Michelle showed up."

Lips pursed, Wanda said nothing.

"I'm wondering if someone at the party gave Eric the cigarettes," said Beanie.

Wanda gave him a sharp scowl. "Someone like me, you mean?"

Shaking his head, Beanie said, "At the party, Eric told me he was going to have a smoke with his friends, Ted, Keith, and Aaron."

Tilting her head, Wanda asked, "You think one of them gave Eric a drug-laced cigarette? That's not possible. Ted, Aaron, and Keith were Eric's best friends. He'd known them all his life. Neither one of them would want to kill Eric. They don't have a motive."

"You don't know that one of them didn't have a motive," said Beanie.

"And you don't know that one of them did," shot back Wanda.

Beanie decided to move on. "Wanda, did you know a man named Melvin Reed?"

"Melvin Reed?" Wanda frowned. "That name doesn't sound familiar. Why? Who is he?"

"So, I'm guessing you don't remember Eric mentioning that name? Melvin Reed?"

Shaking her head, Wanda asked, "Who is Melvin Reed? Is he someone from Eric's past? Do you think he had something to do with Eric's death?"

Beanie sighed. "No, actually … I think Eric knew something about Melvin Reed's death."

"Melvin Reed is dead?"

"He was killed," said Beanie. "Shot twice in the head. It happened in St. Felipe. The police believed Melvin Reed was robbed, but—"

"Why would Eric know anything about some man in St. Felipe who'd been robbed and shot in the head?"

"Eric was from St. Felipe," pointed out Beanie.

"I know, that," said Wanda. "But …"

"But …?" prompted Beanie, wondering why Wanda had trailed off.

"Eric did go to St. Felipe quite a few times last April," said Wanda. "I'm not sure why."

"Did you ask him?" questioned Beanie, at once recalling the conversation he'd overheard between Leon and Wanda at the

Thanksgiving party. Hadn't Leon mentioned following Eric to St. Felipe?

"No, because I figured he was visiting friends or family," said Wanda. "Now I'm wondering if Eric went to see that Melvin Reed guy. Can't imagine why, though, if that's true."

"That's what I'm trying to find out," said Beanie. "I think there might be a connection between Melvin Reed and Eric—"

"You think Eric and this Melvin guy were killed by the same person?"

Beanie said, "I think it's possible. As I said, I think Eric knew something about Melvin's murder. Before Eric died, he asked me to look into a situation for him."

"A situation?"

"He'd been receiving strange emails," said Beanie. "Did you know about that?"

"I had no idea." Wanda looked stricken. "What kind of strange emails?"

"Someone wanted answers from Eric," said Beanie.

"What kind of answers?"

"Eric didn't know," said Beanie. "That's why he wanted me to track down who'd sent the emails and I was able to do that. I think someone named Oscar Reed sent the emails to Eric."

"Oscar Reed?"

"Melvin Reed's son," said Beanie. "Oscar sent emails to Eric. One of the emails had a subject line that said, tell me what happened."

"What happened about what?"

"I don't know this for sure," said Beanie. "But I think Oscar believed that Eric knew something about Melvin Reed's murder."

Wanda jumped up and resumed her pacing. "What could Eric know?"

"Maybe he knew who killed Melvin Reed," said Beanie. "Or maybe—"

"I think you are on the wrong track," said Wanda, eyes flashing in anger.

"I don't agree," said Beanie. "If Eric knew who killed Melvin Reed, then he might have been killed by someone who didn't want that information revealed. The person who killed Melvin Reed might have killed Eric."

Wanda let out a frustrated growl, then stomped back to the couch and dropped down on the flat cushions. "You want to know who killed Eric?"

"You sound like you have an idea," said Beanie.

Wanda leaned forward, her gaze intense. "The PC-5."

Beanie frowned. "Why do you think that?"

Dragging a hand down her face, Wanda said, "I didn't tell the cops this, but … a few months ago, back in September, when Eric and I were still living in Little Turkey, before we moved here, the gang sent some guys to our apartment to threaten Eric…"

32

Later that afternoon, before he headed to his mother-in-law's house to pick up Ethan and Evan, Beanie stopped by the Purple Gecko. There, he asked the bartender, a man whose name he always forgot, if Lime Shoes was available for a chat.

Fifteen minutes later, Beanie found himself in the booth at the back of the bar, where Lime Shoes held court.

The old gangster, a lifelong member of the PC-5, was one of Beanie's more controversial sources.

Beanie met Lime Shoes several years ago, a terrifying experience—for Beanie, at least. Following an article in which Beanie had speculated that PC-5 members had attacked and robbed several elderly Handweg residents, he'd been blindfolded and kidnapped. After a horrifying car ride to a shack in the jungle, Beanie had come face to face with Lime Shoes. The seventy-something gang member explained that the cartel didn't appreciate his speculative editorializing; and that its members didn't viciously attack old women walking home from church services. Beanie had thought he would be forbidden to write about the gang.

On the contrary, Lime Shoes explained that he could write about the PC-5, but he could only publish true and correct facts. No unfounded accusations. No conjecture. In other words, if it was true that the PC-5 was behind a specific crime, then Beanie could write those facts. But if he only suspected the PC-5 was behind a specific crime, then he couldn't print his speculation.

As Lime Shoes put it, the PC-5 would not take credit for crimes it didn't commit. Their relationship, though risky and sometimes nerve-racking, was one Beanie valued. When it came to information about the island cartel, Beanie relied on Lime Shoes for accuracy, if not always honesty.

"I am assuming you did not stop by to inquire about my health and well-being," said Lime Shoes before taking a sip of whiskey.

Beanie chuckled at Lime Shoes' perceptiveness. "How are you?"

"Well, my doctor says my blood pressure is high but other than that." Lime Shoes shrugged, then gave Beanie a shrewd look. "But I doubt you care about my blood pressure. What do you need?"

"Confirmation," said Beanie, ignoring Lime Shoe's baleful glare. The old gangster, he suspected, was fond of him, but couldn't appear weak.

Lime Shoes frowned. "Confirmation about what?"

Beanie repeated Wanda Barnes' story about the PC-5 visiting Eric. "Is that true?"

Lime Shoes fingered his shark's teeth strung on a thin rope around his neck. The rumor was that the old gangster had killed the shark and personally removed each tooth from the beast's mouth. He said, "She didn't lie to you."

"What was the visit about?"

"What did the widow Barnes tell you?"

"She claimed she didn't know," said Beanie. "And said Eric wouldn't tell her. Said it was best if she didn't know."

Lime Shoes said, "The gang had some questions for Barnes about a friend of his who, at the time, was under the investigation by the PIIBs."

"Why was the friend under investigation?"

"This friend had once laundered money for the gang," said Lime Shoes. "The friend had an accounting firm which, from time to time, the cartel sent funds through."

Recalling Eric's gang ties, Beanie rubbed his jaw. "So this friend under investigation was in the PC-5."

"Not an official member," said the old gangster. "An associate. Anyway, the cartel wanted to find out if the friend had revealed any information to Barnes about the friend's operations with the PC-5."

"And had he?"

Lime Shoes sipped more whiskey. "Barnes didn't know anything."

"Who was the friend under investigation?"

"Can't tell you that."

Knowing he might be pushing his luck, Beanie asked, "So, just to confirm, the PC-5 didn't kill Eric?"

Lime Shoes gave Beanie a look.

Chuckling nervously, Beanie said, "I didn't think they had."

33

Caleb said, "Detective Janvier is still convinced that Wanda did it."

Beanie glanced at the most senior reporter, sitting to the right of him at a table in the *Palmchat Gazette* breakroom. Outside the plate glass walls, rain drenched the town, coming down in torrential sheets. The dark clouds and stormy skies made the fluorescent lighting appear brighter at seven in the morning.

Since there hadn't been any urgent, breaking news overnight, Beanie decided to discuss his theories about the Eric Barnes case with Caleb and Sophie.

After a sip of his first cup of coffee of the day, Beanie nodded. "First, Janvier believed she enticed Leon to switch the plastic cups, causing Eric to drink a Palmito made with pineapple juice, thus causing a fatal allergic reaction. But now that the cause of death was a drug overdose Janvier thinks Wanda knew Eric was a secret smoker and she laced his cigarettes with the Vaughn Pharma pain drug. He figures Wanda put them in Eric's pack of cigarettes, knowing that he would secretly smoke one, and when he did, which happened to be at the Thanksgiving party, he would drop dead."

Sophie frowned. "So how does Janvier think Wanda got the Vaughn Pharma pain drug when it's still in development?"

Caleb shook his head. "There's no way she could have gotten it."

"I agree," said Beanie. "But you know how Janvier looks for evidence to support his confirmation bias."

"But there really is no evidence against Wanda," pointed out Sophie.

"Janvier is not going to admit that," said Beanie, taking another sip of coffee. "Not to himself or anyone else."

Grunting, Caleb said, "They need to fire that man."

Sophie said, "What about Michelle Ward? She has a strong motive and means … and a pretty good opportunity. She works at Vaughn Pharma. She could have easily gotten a sample of the new experimental drug."

Beanie said, "She could have laced a few cigarettes with the drug and then given them to Eric."

Caleb frowned. "Would he have accepted cigarettes from an ex-wife he had beef with?"

"Maybe." Sophie said, "She could have done this when they met to talk about the child custody hearing."

"I don't know about that," doubted Caleb.

Sophie asked, "Well, what about the PC-5?"

Caleb said, "The gang is blamed for everything and usually responsible for nothing."

"However, my PC-5 contact told me something very interesting," said Beanie. "The gang paid a visit to Eric a few months ago. They questioned Eric about a friend of his who was being investigated by the PIIB. Apparently, the friend used to launder money for the gang. The cartel wondered if the friend had told Eric anything about the operation."

Caleb frowned. "So, the PC-5 was trying to determine everyone the PIIB might try to talk to. Makes sense."

"Did Eric know anything about the friend's money laundering?" asked Sophie.

Beanie shook his head. "Whoever the friend is—my contact refused to tell me—they didn't spill any PC-5 secrets to Eric."

"Which means the PC-5 probably didn't kill Eric," concluded Sophie.

"Exactly," agreed Beanie. "And the way Eric was killed isn't the way the gang would—"

"Beanie, dude!" Stevie walked into the breakroom, soaking wet, shaking his umbrella, spraying water. "I've been looking for you!"

"What is it?" asked Beanie.

"My cousin got into Eric Barnes' phone," said Stevie, plopping down into a chair at the table. "I got the texts from Michelle. Wanda was right. I think Michelle killed Eric."

"Why?" asked Sophie.

"Listen to these texts Michelle Ward sent to Eric Barnes," said Stevie, fishing a cell phone from the pocket of his board shorts. "'Eric don't do this, please. I will do whatever it takes to stop you and if that means you get hurt, then so be it. Eric, how can you be so cruel and evil? I know you hate me but why would you want to see me suffer like this. You have gone too far and crossed a line and what happens to you is going to be your own fault. I will not lose my kids because of you. I will kill you before I let that happen.'"

Sophie said, "Well, Michelle told Eric she would kill him …"

Caleb said, "And it appears she might have …"

Beanie shook his head. "Yeah, it seems that way, but I don't know."

"What don't you know?" asked Stevie. "Dude, these texts—"

"Michelle could have been trying to scare Eric," said Beanie "Or, maybe she was scared and frustrated and saying things she didn't mean and never intended to do. Look, the texts make Michelle look guilty, but I'm not ready to believe she killed Eric."

"Why not?" asked Caleb.

Beanie finished his coffee and then told his coworkers about Oscar and Melvin Reed.

Beanie said, "I'm starting to wonder if Eric was killed because he knew too much. Maybe he knew who killed Melvin Reed."

Sophie asked, "And you think Melvin Reed's son, Oscar, emailed Eric because he thought Eric knew who'd killed Melvin?"

Beanie said, "Or, maybe not who killed Melvin, but maybe something about his death. Like, maybe Eric knew that Melvin had been targeted after he'd gone to the bank."

Caleb asked, "But how did Oscar come to the conclusion that Eric knew something about Melvin's death?"

Beanie said, "That I don't know. That's why I want to talk to Oscar. Because I realize that Oscar might not have been emailing Eric about Melvin's murder."

Stevie said, "Oscar might not have even emailed Eric."

Sophie agreed. "As you said, first you need to confirm if Oscar sent the messages to Eric. And if so, then you can ask Oscar what he thought Eric knew."

Beanie nodded. "Yeah, I know. Problem is, I'm having trouble locating Oscar. But I'm hoping he'll contact me. I have a feeling he might be the key to figuring out who killed Eric."

34

"You are taking those texts out of context," said Michelle Ward.

After his conversation with Caleb, Sophie, and Stevie, Beanie called Michelle.

Beanie said, "I think the context of ... *'I will not lose my kids because of you. I will kill you before I let that happen'* ... is pretty clear."

"What I meant was, when I texted Eric, I was desperate and afraid," said Michelle. "I wasn't thinking straight. I didn't mean that I would really kill Eric. I would never kill him. I don't want to go to prison. Killing Eric would ensure that I would lose my kids."

"And now that Eric is dead, you probably won't lose your children."

"You know what, you're right," said Michelle. "I suppose it looks like Eric's death is convenient for me, but that's not the truth. You know why? Because Eric was going to tell the judge lies about me! He was being vindictive. I don't deserve to have my kids taken away from me! I am a good mother!"

Not interested in Michelle's passionate defense of her motherly instincts, Beanie said, "So, I'm sure you heard about how Eric really died. It wasn't an allergic reaction."

"I never thought it was," said Michelle.

"It was the experimental Vaughn Pharma pain drug," said Beanie.

There was silence on the other end of the line.

"So now the cops have to figure out how that drug, which is still in development and not even on the market yet, ended up in a cigarette Eric smoked at the Thanksgiving party," said Beanie. "They need to find out who gave Eric the cigarette."

"What makes the police think someone gave Eric the cigarette?" asked Michelle. "Maybe he signed up for the drug protocol. I told you Eric had back issues."

"The protocols for the drug haven't started yet, which I'm sure you know," said Beanie. "The drug was obtained by someone with access to the labs at Vaughn Pharma."

"Someone like me, you mean," said Michelle.

"You work for Vaughn Pharma," said Beanie.

"I'm not on the team developing that particular drug," said Michelle.

"But I'm sure you could have gotten your hands on some of it," said Beanie. "Just like you got the fentanyl you took from the company."

"That is not true," said Michelle. "I never stole any fentanyl. That sick, malicious rumor was started by people at the company who don't like me, and if you put that in the paper, I will sue you!"

"There's no need to call your lawyers," said Beanie. "I'm not interested in assassinating your character. I just want to know if any samples have gone missing from the company. You would know that, right?"

Michelle sighed. "I haven't heard anything."

Beanie said, "Well if you do, can you—"

The line went dead.

Confused by the buzzing dial tone, Beanie said, "Hello? Michelle are you there?"

Seconds later, he hung up. He turned to his computer and opened a Word file, intent on typing notes from the conversation while they were still fresh in his mind. As soon as he placed his fingers on the keyboard, his desk phone rang again.

Hoping it was Michelle Ward calling to tell him they'd accidentally been disconnected, Beanie grabbed the receiver. "Roland Bean."

"Hey, it's Fields. You got a minute?"

"Of course," said Beanie. "What's going on?"

"Did I tell you that the chief assigned Janvier a new partner? Detective Joshua Jones."

"Don't think you mentioned it."

"Well, Janvier and Jones … we call 'em J&J … almost came to blows," said Fields, his voice lowered.

"What? Why?"

"Jones is getting frustrated with Janvier," said Fields. "The man is like a dog with a bone when it comes to pinning Eric's murder on Wanda, even though it's looking like he's targeting the wrong wife."

"What do you mean?"

"Jones found out that the experimental drug—it's called methachloride, by the way—is being developed by a Vaughn Pharma team that Michelle Ward is overseeing."

"Wait, what?" Beanie stopped typing. "Michelle is on the team working on the new drug."

"She pretty much created the new drug," said Fields. "Which means she had exclusive access. But, Janvier is not convinced, for whatever reason."

"I just spoke to Michelle Ward," said Beanie. "She told me she wasn't on the team."

"Yeah, that's what she told Jones, too," said Fields. "After he found out she'd lied, she refused to talk to him. Said he would have to send a formal request to the Vaughn Pharma lawyers if he wanted to interview her again."

Beanie rubbed his jaw. "She hung up on me."

"Jones thinks she's hiding something," said Fields.

"I agree," said Beanie. "Maybe the fact that she gave Eric the drug-laced cigarette that killed him."

35

"Reporter Bean, how many times do I have to tell you," began Detective Janvier. "I do not need, nor do I want your help. I am perfectly capable of investigating the murder of Eric Barnes without your assistance."

Fighting frustration, Beanie squirmed in his seat. The last place he wanted to be was sitting on the opposite side of Janvier's desk in the detective's office at seven in the morning. But he'd decided the threatening text messages from Michelle that Stevie's hacker cousin had found on Eric's phone were important enough to risk dealing with the irascible lawman.

After a deep, fortifying breath, Beanie said, "I really think you should take the text messages into consideration."

Janvier sighed. "Even if I wanted to, and trust me I do not, I could not use the text messages because they were, most likely, illegally obtained. I am aware that your newspaper employs a mysterious hacker, no? Well, hacking into the cell phone of the victim is illegal. I can't use those texts to arrest Michelle Ward. Any half-decent low-rent defense attorney would get that evidence tossed."

Beanie asked, "But now that you know about the texts, can't you launch your own investigation? Can't you subpoena Eric Barnes' cell phone records?"

"Of course, I could," said Janvier. "But I will not."

"Why am I not surprised?"

"Threatening to kill someone is not the same thing as killing someone," said Janvier. "There must be evidence that connects a suspect to the murder."

"Well, if you would investigate Michelle, you might find the evidence," said Beanie. "Eric Barnes was killed with a drug-laced cigarette. Michelle Ward works as a research scientist for Vaughn Pharma where she headed the team that was developing the new pain drug, and—"

"Reporter Bean, I am aware of Michelle Ward's credentials," said Janvier.

"Are you aware that she lied to your partner, Jones?" asked Beanie. "She told him that she wasn't working on the new pain drug, and—"

"I am aware," said Janvier, chin lifted, gaze haughty. "I know you believe you are a clever investigator, but you have given me nothing that I don't already know. Now, I have work to do, so—"

"Did you know that Michelle Ward gave Eric a fentanyl patch?"

Janvier's eyes narrowed. "And you know this how?"

Beanie told him.

Janvier shook his head. "That is akin to hearsay. Right now, you are telling me about a statement you overheard, one which can easily be disputed, and because Eric Barnes is dead, it becomes your word against Michelle Ward's about the fentanyl patches."

"She was accused of stealing fentanyl from the company to sell it," said Beanie. "She was trying to finance her divorce."

His gaze shrewd, Janvier asked, "And you know that how?"

Beanie sighed. "Again, it's hearsay, but I spoke to a receptionist at Vaughn Pharma. You could take the receptionist's statement. You could talk to HR at Vaughn Pharma."

"And they would tell me nothing." Janvier sneered. "Refer me to their legal department who would object to each and every one of my inquiries. No thanks. Just tell me what the receptionist told you."

Beanie was shocked. "What?"

"Tell me what the receptionist told you," repeated Janvier.

"You want to know?" Beanie was suspicious. Was Janvier really asking for information from him?

Janvier frowned. "Reporter Bean, have you suddenly lost the ability to understand English? Should I repeat my request in patois?"

Beanie returned the frown. "That won't be necessary," he said, then recounted the receptionist's story.

Janvier stroked his chin. "In light of the information you just imparted, I am willing to entertain the idea that Michelle Ward may have had a hand in the death of her ex-husband."

"I think it's entirely plausible," said Beanie. "Michelle had motive and means."

"What about opportunity?" asked Janvier.

Chagrined, Beanie said, "Well, that's going to be difficult to prove."

"On the contrary," said Janvier. "Michelle Ward had an opportunity to kill Eric Barnes. But … not alone."

"I don't understand," said Beanie.

"Michelle Ward would have had to have help to kill her ex-husband," said Janvier. "She needed someone to give Eric Barnes this deadly cigarette."

"So you think what?" asked Beanie, struggling to follow the detective's logic, which he suspected was faulty. "That Michelle brought the cigarette to the Thanksgiving party and gave it to someone to give to Eric?"

"I believe that is exactly what happened," said Janvier, his tone pompous.

"Any idea who?" asked Beanie, not convinced of the detective's theory.

"Wanda Barnes."

36

The next day, sipping his second cup of coffee that morning, Beanie leaned back in the leather chair behind the desk in his small cubicle at the *Palmchat Gazette*.

Since his conversation with Detective Philippi Janvier yesterday afternoon, Beanie had been pondering the idea of Wanda Barnes and Michelle Ward working together to get rid of Eric Barnes. Janvier's theory. Beanie thought the misguided detective was completely off base.

Janvier believed Wanda had been sick of Eric, or not in love with him, and wanted to get rid of him. She wanted her husband dead so she could collect a sizeable insurance settlement. The same way she'd collected insurance funds from her first husband, whose family suspected she'd had a hand in the man's death. According to Janvier, Wanda had a pattern. So she conspired with Michelle, who also wanted Eric dead so he couldn't testify against her.

The two wives of Eric Barnes worked together to ensure his demise if Janvier was to be believed.

Which Beanie thought he wasn't.

Beanie drummed his fingers against the tiny desk in his small cubicle. Janvier's theory was ridiculous. There was no way Beanie could get behind it. First of all, Wanda and Michelle hated each other. Beanie doubted the women could get along long enough to kill Eric. They would have ended up killing each other.

Second of all, there was no evidence connecting Wanda to the murder. She had no access to the experimental Vaughn Pharma pain drug. Her fingerprints hadn't been found on the drug-laced cigarette that killed Eric. She should have been cleared of suspicion by now, and she would have been if Janvier could admit he was wrong.

Michelle Ward was a much more likely suspect.

And yet, Beanie couldn't stop thinking about Oscar Reed and the 'coolkidstable' emails sent to Eric.

The idea that Eric's death was somehow connected to Marvin Reed's death still intrigued Beanie. He wanted to investigate and explore the possibility. Beanie sighed and took another sip of coffee. He needed to talk to Oscar Reed. First, he had to find the guy. Both his mother and his former roommate, Ash, had promised to contact Beanie if they'd heard from Oscar.

Beanie contemplated reaching out to Ash or Heather Reed. He turned to his computer to compose an email to Ash, and—

"Hey, got a tip for you!"

Beanie glanced over his shoulder.

His coworker, Sophie Carter, bounded into the cubicle, wearing a dress the color of cotton candy, excitement in her brown eyes as she plopped down in the chair in front of Beanie's desk.

Swiveling in his squeaky leather chair, Beanie faced his bubbly coworker. "About what?"

Sophie smiled. "The Eric Barnes case …"

"You found out something?"

"You know Landon George, right?" asked Sophie. "My friend who works at Dizzy Jenny's?"

Leaning back, Beanie stared at Sophie.

He knew Landon George, and what he knew he didn't exactly like.

George, a handsome, young bartender at Dizzy Jenny's, was a PC-5 liaison. Though not in the island cartel, he functioned as a mob ambassador, of sorts, bridging the gap between the gang and those who wished to secretly employ the gang's services.

In the past, George had provided information to both Vivian and Sophie, solidifying himself as an unofficial source for the paper, which Beanie didn't mind. What bothered him was Sophie's insistence on defining Landon George as her friend. Beanie didn't trust the guy. And he didn't believe that George wasn't in the gang.

But he knew he couldn't throw stones, considering his wife's former past with the island cartel. Still, Beanie thought of Sophie as a little sister. Landon George was dangerous, and Beanie was sure Sophie found the element of danger exciting and thrilling.

After all, whenever Sophie mentioned Landon, her face lit up. Beanie didn't want her to get hurt—emotionally, or physically.

"What about him?" asked Beanie, trying to hide his interest. Just because he didn't like George didn't mean he wasn't champing at the bit to find out what the guy might know. Much like Lime Shoes, Landon George could be counted on to provide crucial information.

"Landon told me that he remembers Eric Barnes coming into Dizzy Jenny's with some guy," said Sophie. "And before you ask, Landon brought up Eric Barnes. I wasn't trying to poach your story."

"Did I accuse you?" asked Beanie, not sure if he should be offended.

Tilting her head, Sophie gave him a look. "Beanie, you know how protective you get about your stories."

Beanie shrugged. Sophie was right. He was, at times, proprietary, but the news business was competitive. He would collaborate when he had to, nevertheless, he was trying to build a brand—one he wasn't necessarily inclined to share.

"Anyway, because I know you'll return the favor, I will hip you to the jive."

Beanie snorted a laugh. "Hip me to the jive?"

Sophie giggled. "My grandma said that to me the other day.

Apparently, it was popular slang back in the day. Anyhoo, Landon said Eric and the guy were having an intense conversation. Looked like an argument."

"An argument," said Beanie, wondering who Eric might have been arguing with. "What did the guy look like?"

"Landon said typical Avalon Estates guy," said Sophie, shrugging. "European, probably. Well-dressed. And there was something about the guy's credit card."

"What about it?" asked Beanie.

"I don't remember," said Sophie, looking sheepish. "Me and Landon had this conversation a few days ago, which is when I meant to tell you, but I forgot because Viv sent me out to cover the latest Little Turkey protest."

Beanie nodded. "Great article, by the way."

Sophie beamed. "Thanks. It was intense. But I understand why the residents took to the streets. The smell from that new landfill is horrible. No one should be expected to live with air that foul."

"What is the company going to do about it?" asked Beanie.

"Not sure," said Sophie. "They're not commenting. They haven't even given an official statement. And the mayor's office is kicking the can and passing the buck. Hopefully, the company will do the right thing and deal with the smell."

"Hopefully," agreed Beanie, thankful that Oyster Farms, though not one of St. Killian's prosperous, high-end neighborhoods, didn't suffer the same problems as Little Turkey.

Exhaling, Sophie said, "So … you want to go and talk to Landon about Eric Barnes?"

37

An hour later, Beanie followed Sophie into Dizzy Jenny's, the popular beachfront restaurant, renowned for its fresh seafood and lively atmosphere.

At one in the afternoon, the restaurant did brisk business. Every available table was taken, occupied by tourists and residents. Waiters scurried and snaked between the tables, carrying platters of food and drinks above their heads. A boisterous din of conversation mixed with the jaunty calypso beat floated through the air.

Beanie walked with Sophie to the end of the U-shaped bar, where glamourous, well-dressed patrons drank pastel-colored cocktails garnished with fresh fruit as they participated in seeing and being seen.

"I just got a text from Landon," said Sophie, who'd texted the liaison while Beanie drove them to the restaurant. "He's got a break in ten minutes and then he'll talk to us."

Fifteen minutes later, Landon George met them at the bar, then suggested they talk outside the restaurant, near the rear employee parking lot. Standing beneath the paltry shade of a cluster of palm trees, Beanie greeted George with curt, terse pleasantries.

Sophie donned sunglasses, then said, "So, I told Beanie what you told me about Eric Barnes."

"I've been reading your stories," said Landon. "When I saw the photo of the guy who died—Eric Barnes—I realized I'd seen him in here."

"And when was this?"

"About two weeks before he died," said Landon. "Came in here with a white guy. Nicely dressed, like he'd stepped off a yacht."

"Did you recognize the guy?"

Landon shook his head. "He wasn't a regular. I'd never seen him come in here before."

Beanie asked, "And Eric was arguing with the guy?"

"Looked that way to me," said Landon. "Eric Barnes kept putting his finger in the guy's face, but the guy wasn't really reacting. Seemed to be trying to calm Eric down."

"You didn't happen to hear any of the argument?" asked Sophie.

"I was at the bar at the time," said Landon. "Not too far away, but it was busy. Hard to hear anything when we got a packed house."

Nodding, Beanie wondered if maybe it would be better to talk with the waiter who'd served Eric and the mystery companion. Provided Landon remembered the waiter. Or, if he even knew. Might be worth a try to ask and—

"Eventually, Eric Barnes got up and left," said Landon. "Threw his napkin down and walked away."

"Intense," said Sophie. "Wonder what the argument was about?"

Beanie asked, "Sophie mentioned you said there was something weird about a credit card?" Landon said, "The guy Eric argued with paid with a credit card, which he ended up forgetting at the restaurant. The waiter mentioned to me that the guy left his credit card. He wondered what to do, so I told him I would take care of it, so he could get back to his tables. It was a company card, I remember that."

"What company?"

"That I don't remember," said Landon. "But I called the company and asked for the name on the card. The receptionist told me that the guy whose name was on the card no longer owned the business."

Beanie frowned. "That's weird."

Landon nodded. "So I asked the receptionist if she had a new number for the guy."

Sophie asked, "And did she?"

Shaking his head, Landon said, "She told me the guy was dead."

"Dead?" echoed Sophie.

Beanie scratched his chin. "The guy paid for his lunch with a business card that belonged to a dead guy."

"Must have been a stolen card," said Landon. "That's what I figured. So, I threw the card in the restaurant's lost and found. Figured the guy might come back for the card."

Sophie shook her head. "If the card was stolen, I doubt he's coming back for it. He probably didn't intend to use it again."

Beanie asked, "Did the charges go through on the card?"

Landon nodded. "Yeah. Otherwise, the waiter would have gone back to the guy and told him the card was declined."

"So the dead man's business card is still active," said Beanie.

"Odd," said Sophie.

Sighing, Beanie said, "Maybe the man died recently. His family or estate rep might be in the process of making arrangements to close his accounts."

"Still doesn't explain why the guy was using the credit card of a dead man," said Sophie. "Unless he didn't know the guy was dead. Maybe he stole the card before the guy died."

Beanie asked, "And I'm guessing you don't remember the name on the card?"

"No, but the card is still here," said Landon. "The guy didn't come back for it. You want to see it?"

Beanie nodded.

As Landon headed back into the restaurant, Sophie asked, "Strange, huh?"

"Very," agreed Beanie.

Ten minutes later, Landon returned with the business card.

Beanie stared at the name embossed on the plastic.

A sharp jolt sliced through him.

The card, issued by VISA, bore the name …

MELVIN REED

38

Gripping the wheel of his SUV, Beanie frowned.

Surrounded by vehicles, he glanced at the dashboard clock—5:37 p.m. He was due to pick up Ethan and Evan from Noelle's mom's house in Handweg, but traffic was a nightmare. He doubted he would make it on time, and he didn't know why. Sighing, he grabbed his phone. Checking an island traffic app, he discovered the backup was due to an accident miles ahead. The app projected maybe another half hour before the wreck was cleared and traffic started moving again. Beanie texted his mother-in-law to let her know he'd be late, which wasn't a problem with her as she loved spending as much time with her grandsons as possible.

With traffic at a standstill, Beanie shifted into 'park,' and reflected on the conversation with Landon George.

To say he'd been shook was an understatement.

An image of the business card floated into his head. Again, he saw the embossed name: Melvin Reed. Oscar's father. The man who'd been killed in St. Felipe. Shot twice in the head and dumped behind a daycare center for innocent children to find.

He still couldn't fathom it. Hours of rampant speculation with

Sophie hadn't provided any clarity. Beanie still didn't know what to think.

Why had Eric been talking to a guy who had a credit card that belonged to Melvin Reed? Who was the man Eric had argued with at Dizzy Jenny's? Why did that man have Melvin Reed's credit card? How did the mystery man know Melvin Reed?

Nothing made sense.

Except that there was a connection between Eric Barnes and Melvin Reed. But what was the connection? Beanie wasn't sure. He suspected, however, that Eric had known something about Melvin Reed's death. And maybe the man he'd argued with had known something about Melvin Reed's death as well. Maybe that man had robbed Melvin Reed? The mystery man who'd used Melvin Reed's credit card might have killed him, then taken his wallet and the money Reed had withdrawn from the bank.

Beanie wondered if Eric and the mystery man had argued about Melvin Reed's death. Maybe Eric was tired of keeping the man's secret. Maybe Eric had threatened to expose the mystery man. And then, maybe—

The cell phone chirped, signaling a call.

Answering, Beanie said, "Roland Bean ..."

"It's Michelle Ward ..."

Surprised, Beanie said, "Michelle. How are you?"

"I'll be doing a lot better if we can have a conversation," said Michelle.

Picking up on a shrill nervousness in Michelle's tone, Beanie asked, "A conversation about ...?"

"Eric's murder," said Michelle. "I have some information. I know who killed Eric."

Beanie exhaled. "Then you should probably be having that conversation with the police."

"I don't trust the cops," said Michelle, her voice rising. "The police can't help me."

"Michelle, I really think—"

"I want to tell you who killed Eric," said Michelle. "But I can't have this conversation over the phone."

Scoffing, Beanie said, "Of course not."

"I want to be videotaped," said Michelle. "You can do one of those live interactive stories."

"Okay …" said Beanie, not convinced that Michelle was entirely on the level. "When do you want to meet?"

"Tonight," she said. "Right now. I want this story out in the public as soon as possible."

Knowing that his mother-in-law wouldn't mind keeping the boys a bit longer, Beanie asked, "Why the urgency?"

Michelle said, "Because the person who killed Eric won't kill me if the world knows the truth …"

39

After entering Michelle Ward's address in the SUV's GPS, Beanie followed the directions of the disembodied voice leading him to Allegra Shores, where Eric's ex-wife lived.

His mind racing, Beanie clutched the steering wheel.

Michelle Ward claimed she knew who killed Eric.

Initially, Beanie had been floored. After several minutes of processing her announcement, he now had doubts. How did she know? Had she figured it out? Or, had she known all along?

His thoughts shifted to the reason she'd given him for revealing Eric's killer.

The person who killed Eric won't kill me if the world knows the truth.

Michelle was afraid that Eric's killer would come after her. Which meant … what? Eric's killer knew that Michelle was aware of his identity. How did the killer know that? Had Michelle confronted the killer with her knowledge? Why would she have done something so dangerous?

Sighing, Beanie followed a curving, palm-lined lane and then turned right into the two-lane entrance of Allegra Shores.

A feeling of déjà vu washed over him. He'd visited this

neighborhood when he interviewed Eric's friend, Aaron. At the time, Aaron had told him Michelle was crazy. A bitter, vindictive woman who'd killed her second husband. But Aaron didn't believe Michelle had killed Eric, despite having a strong motive for murder. Aaron thought Wanda had killed her husband for the insurance money. Could Aaron have been right? Had Wanda killed Eric?

Initially, Michelle hadn't suspected Wanda. But maybe Michelle had discovered new evidence that proved Wanda's guilt? Beanie couldn't imagine that Wanda had been lying all this time. Couldn't imagine that Janvier's theory had been right. But if Michelle wasn't going to reveal Wanda as the killer, then who?

Beanie thought of the mystery guy who'd argued with Eric at Dizzy Jenny's. The man who'd used Melvin Reed's credit card. Was it possible that he'd killed Eric? Maybe because Eric knew the mystery guy had killed Melvin?

Beanie didn't know. And he decided not to bother trying to guess what Michelle would tell him. He'd arrive at her house soon enough and when they spoke, he would know for sure … or, would he?

Beanie exited the coastal highway and entered a traffic circle.

Part of him wondered if he was walking into a hoax. Or, worse, a trap. Michelle might be trying to fool him. But, if so, why? What could she gain by luring him to her home with the promise of revealing Eric's killer if she didn't know who killed him?

His heart pounding, Beanie gripped the wheel tighter as the navigation system guided him through the streets. Driving through the neighborhood of expensive homes with the fading sunlight streaming into the car, casting a coppery glow over the dashboard and instrument panel, Beanie turned onto Michelle's street. Decreasing his speed, Beanie approached his destination. Surrounded by lush vegetation and rows of large, thick Oleander bushes that served as privacy between the neighbors, the house appeared dark.

Slowing to a stop in front of the curving driveway, Beanie stared at the light-colored Audi SUV parked in front of the three-car garage.

Relieved that Michelle was home, he pulled in behind her car and cut the engine. Outside in the balmy atmosphere, he hurried past the Audi and walked to the front door.

Standing in the alcove, Beanie rang the doorbell several times. Minutes later, when there was no response, Beanie knocked on the door. He frowned. Why wasn't Michelle answering the door? For a moment, he wondered if she wasn't home. But, no, her car was in the driveway. And she'd known he was coming to talk to her. She'd asked him to meet her.

Exhaling, Beanie rang the doorbell again. From her shrill, frantic tone on the phone, Beanie had thought she would be waiting outside the house, or standing in the driveway.

Fighting frustration, Beanie glanced over his shoulder.

He frowned.

The passenger door of the Audi was open. What was that about? How had the passenger door gotten open? Who had opened it? Had someone been in the car?

"Michelle …" Beanie called out. Leaving the alcove, he walked toward the Audi. From a few feet away, he glanced at the front windshield. He couldn't see anyone in the car. Apprehensive, Beanie headed around to the passenger side. Stepping into the space of the opened door, Beanie bent over and looked into the car.

A shudder passed through him.

"Oh my God …"

Slumped over the bucket seat was Michelle Ward, blood seeping from a gaping hole above her right ear.

"Michelle …" Beanie's heart shot into his throat. "Oh my God … Michelle …"

Cautiously, Beanie leaned into the car and pressed two fingers against her neck. Her skin was warm, but there was no pulse. Beanie maneuvered out of the car. Shock coursed through his body. He didn't understand. Didn't know what to think.

Michelle Ward was dead.

Beanie took a deep breath. He needed to call the police. With trembling fingers, he shoved a hand into the pocket of his Dockers to get his phone and—

Something snapped.

Startled, Beanie glanced around. As he tried to identify the sound, and the direction it had come from, he heard more thrashing and snapping. Ahead, near the thick, leafy hibiscus trees near the garage, the branches rustled, as though something, or someone, was moving through them.

Peering toward the tangle of privacy bushes on the side of the house, Beanie saw someone running through the thick, overgrown Oleander trees planted along the side of the house.

"Hey!" Beanie cried out, his gaze focused on the figure pushing through the tall shrubs. "Stop!"

Without thinking, Beanie took off after the retreating figure. "You! Stop!"

Pushing through the bushes and shrubs, Beanie struggled to keep the person in sight as they ran along the side of the house. Everything within Beanie told him to abandon the pursuit. He had no doubt he was following the person who'd killed Michelle—the person who'd killed Eric. It was a dangerous, and foolish, endeavor. But he couldn't stand there and let the killer get away, could he? Not when he had a chance to find out who had—

Beanie's ankle rolled as he stepped on something underfoot. Cursing under his breath, feeling himself tripping, he stumbled. Beanie grabbed an Oleander branch, trying to stop his fall. With a fistful of flowers and leaves, he lost his balance. Somehow, he stopped from falling by managing to take a knee in the ankle-high grass. Cursing again, Beanie staggered to his feet, pulse racing …

Ahead, the privacy shrubs bent and swayed under the assault of the killer, steadily and quickly fleeing the scene.

Taking a deep breath, Beanie glanced down, trying to figure out what he'd tripped over.

A few inches away from his foot, he spotted it.

Was that a …

Beanie crouched down.

In the waning sunlight, he stared at something that seemed familiar to him for some reason:

A large neon green shoe …

40

"Eric's killer killed Michelle Ward," said Stevie. "But who is the killer? And why did Eric's killer kill her?"

Beanie took a sip of coffee and glanced at his coworkers, Stevie, Sophie, and Caleb, sitting with him at a table in the breakroom.

Three days had passed since Beanie had discovered Michelle Ward's dead body, slumped over in the driver's seat of her SUV. After giving his statement to the police who'd first responded, he'd been instructed to stick around until the detective in charge showed up. Though Beanie had hoped to deal with a different detective, he hadn't been surprised when a late model sedan pulled up in front of the house and Janvier got out.

"Michelle was killed because she knew too much," said Beanie, taking a sip of his first cup of coffee that morning.

Popping a donut hole in her mouth, Sophie said, "She knew who killed Eric."

"I don't know why she didn't just tell you," grumbled Caleb. "Then you would know."

"She didn't want to tell me over the phone," said Beanie.

Sophie rolled her eyes. "What's wrong with telling you over the phone? Not to speak ill of the dead, but why did she have to be so melodramatic? What? Did she think she was in a soap opera or something?"

Stevie said, "Maybe she thought she was in a mystery novel?"

Caleb shook his head. "She was so busy being mysterious and ended up dying mysteriously."

Sophie said, "Have you heard anything from the cops about suspects?"

Beanie shook his head. "Which is not surprising. Janvier is not going to give me a comment."

"Who do you think did it?" asked Stevie.

Beanie leaned forward. "Did I tell you guys Janvier's theory about Wanda and Michelle?"

His coworkers shook their heads.

Beanie told them.

Sophie said, "So … you think Wanda killed Michelle to stop her from telling the police about their diabolical plot?"

"But why would Michelle go to the cops if their diabolical plot worked?" asked Stevie. "She wanted him dead. Wanda wanted him dead. He died. No need for Michelle to snitch to the police."

"No honor among thieves," said Caleb. "Or murderous wives."

Beanie nodded. "Those two women couldn't stand each other. I'm not surprised if they fell out over Eric's murder."

Sophie asked, "What if Michelle wanted a cut of the insurance money?"

Beanie said, "That's possible. Michelle was trying to make sure she didn't lose her kids. Wanda was trying to get an insurance settlement. But Michelle was going broke trying to pay for her divorce. She might have felt entitled to some of the insurance money. But Wanda didn't agree."

Stevie said, "So maybe Michelle threatened to tell the cops and Wanda killed her?"

Grabbing another donut hole, Sophie said, "Maybe."

Beanie took a sip of coffee, then said, "Possible, but not probable."

Sophie shrugged. "Okay, then, besides Wanda, who else could have killed Michelle?"

Beanie said, "I was thinking about the guy Eric argued with at Dizzy Jenny's."

Stevie asked, "What about him?"

Sophie popped another donut hole into her mouth. "Why would he kill Michelle Ward?"

"Maybe Michelle knew what Eric and the mystery guy were arguing about," said Beanie. "Maybe she knew that the mystery guy killed Eric."

"But you have no idea what they were arguing about," said Caleb. "Could have been the price of goat in St. Basil, for all you know."

Beanie shook his head. "I think they were arguing about Melvin Reed."

Sophie said, "The dead guy whose credit card the mystery guy with Eric used?"

"Melvin Reed is the father of Oscar Reed," reminded Beanie. "Oscar sent the emails to Eric Barnes."

"But you don't know that for sure," said Caleb.

"Right," agreed Beanie. "But I need to find out."

41

"Janvier is looking at Michelle Ward's widower—Charles Ward—as a possible suspect," said Officer Damon Fields.

At two in the afternoon, he sat across from Fields at a bistro table in the palm tree dining park at Pourciau Square.

Beanie took a sip of coffee, then asked, "What evidence does Janvier have against Ward?"

Fields sighed. "Well, Ward doesn't have an alibi for the day and time of Michelle Ward's death. Says he was at home alone."

"Where were the kids?" asked Beanie.

"With their grandparents," said Fields. "Janvier spoke with them. Ward dropped them off around eight in the morning and didn't pick them up until one in the afternoon the next day."

Beanie nodded. "Gives him plenty of time to kill Michelle."

"Another thing—he recently bought a gun. Four days before Michelle was shot to death, actually. And, apparently, Ward threatened Michelle in public. At the big Island Mart grocery store near the marina."

"He threatened her in public?"

"Witnesses heard him say he would make her pay and she would be sorry," said Fields, shaking his head. "Pretty heated argument. Store security had to break it up. Cops were called. No one was arrested but there was an incident report."

"Is Ward's gun the murder weapon?"

"Janvier is hoping to determine that," said Fields. "We'll see, but I doubt it."

"You don't think Ward did it?"

Fields sat back in his chair. "You know I always think Janvier is on the wrong track. But, who knows? If ballistics shows that Charles Ward's gun is the murder weapon and if we get his DNA from the shoe—"

"The shoe," said Beanie, recalling the object he'd seen in the grass. "I meant to ask you about that."

"Crime scene techs found blood on the shoe," said Fields. "It belonged to the victim, Michelle Ward. They also recovered male sweat DNA from the shoe, which matches male DNA found in the car."

Beanie took out his phone and opened his notetaking app.

Fields went on, "Janvier believes the killer sat in the car with Michelle Ward, shot her, then got out of the car and ran into the bushes."

"Did Michelle have camera surveillance?" asked Beanie.

"Surprisingly, no," said Fields. "But a few of her neighbors across the street had cameras. Janvier is trying to get that surveillance. Might show the killer getting out of the car but I doubt we'll get a clear view. Anyway, I'm hoping Janvier will rely on the shoe evidence."

"I'm guessing Janvier talked to Charles Ward about the shoe?"

"Ward said it wasn't his," said Fields. "Said he'd never seen a shoe like that before. And, he said it wasn't his size. The shoe was a size fifteen. Charles Ward wears a size eleven."

"Did Janvier get DNA from Charles Ward?"

Fields nodded. "Charles Ward offered his DNA to prove, according to him, that he didn't kill Michelle. We haven't gotten the results yet, but when we do, I'll let you know."

42

"Do you believe Charles Ward killed Michelle?" asked Noelle.

As his wife handed him a dirty dish, Beanie eased it into the soapy water and used a scouring sponge to remove remnants of the night's dinner—stewed goat over mashed plantains. With the boys in bed, having been bathed and read to, he and Noelle were tidying up the kitchen before turning in.

"I actually do," said Beanie, recalling his conversation with the man who should have been Michelle's ex-husband but was now her widower.

Following his afternoon coffee break with Officer Fields, Beanie had returned to the paper, grabbed a granola bar from the breakroom, and looked up Charles Ward's contact information, obtained from the incident report Fields had emailed him.

After introducing himself, Beanie's first request had been a comment regarding Michelle Ward's death. He had not asked Charles Ward if he'd killed his wife, but the man's first words were: "I did not kill my wife." Ward's ardent denial sounded dishonest, and yet, somehow, Beanie believed him.

"What do the cops think?" asked Noelle, drying dishes Beanie had finished cleaning.

"They're waiting for the DNA evidence to come back," said Beanie, sinking two smudged glasses into the water. "The guy acknowledges he looks guilty. He and Michelle were in a bitter divorce. Fighting a contentious custody battle. But he said he didn't want her dead."

Noelle asked, "Then why did he buy a gun? Why did he threaten her in public?"

"Ward claimed the gun was for protection," said Beanie. "Claimed Michelle threatened him."

"She threatened him?"

"She threatened him first, according to him," said Beanie, remembering Ward's account.

"Michelle threatened all her husbands," Ward had said. "She was a very volatile woman and that is not me speaking ill of the dead. That is me telling the truth. She killed her second husband, did you know that?"

Beanie said, "She told me it was self-defense."

Charles Ward snorted. "Self-defense my pinky toe. Michelle was never on the defense. She was all offense. She probably killed Eric Barnes, too. He was willing to testify for me so Michelle got rid of him."

"And then someone got rid of her," said Beanie.

"Well, it wasn't me," said Ward.

Exhaling, Beanie grabbed the last plate. "I think I believed him because he admitted that he could not stand Michelle. Said he didn't know what he ever saw in her. Said he never should have married her."

"And yet he did," said Noelle, taking the dried dishes to one of the overhead cabinets. "And had kids with her."

"Ward said the kids were the only good thing that came from their relationship," said Beanie. "The kids are the reason why Ward said he would never kill Michelle. He said their mother's death has destroyed them. They haven't stopped crying."

"That's horrible," said Noelle, leaning against the counter. "Such a terrible tragedy. I am heartbroken for those kids because I can't help but think about what Ethan and Evan would have gone through if—"

"Babe, don't think it, okay?" Beanie abandoned the last dish, rinsed, and dried his hands, then crossed the kitchen to his wife.

"I know I shouldn't," said Noelle, her eyes brimming with tears. "But, we could have lost you."

"But, you didn't lose me," said Beanie, pulling his wife in his arms. "And you won't lose me."

"You promise?" whispered Noelle.

Holding his wife close as she leaned her head against his chest, Beanie said, "I promise."

Sniffing, Noelle eased from his embrace and stepped back. "Roland, do you promise that you won't put yourself in any more dangerous situations where you could be seriously hurt or … even killed?"

Distressed by the sadness in Noelle's gaze, Beanie said, "Don't worry, okay, babe."

"How can I not worry?" asked Noelle. "It's not just that you were stabbed, which was my fault—"

"That was not your fault, please don't think—"

"You were almost burned to death," said Noelle. "You've been shot at more times than I can count and I just—"

"Noelle, listen to me," said Beanie, pulling his wife back into his arms, eager to calm her fears before they got out of control. "I'll be fine, okay? After all, I have a beautiful wife and two bad little boys that I adore. I have everything to live for. Trust me, there is no way I'm getting myself killed."

43

"Charles Ward didn't kill Michelle Ward," said Officer Damon Fields.

Sitting at his tiny desk in his small cubicle, Beanie pressed the 'Speaker' function on his desk phone and replaced the receiver in the cradle. Two days had passed since Fields had given him information regarding Janvier's suspicion of Charles Ward.

"So he's been cleared?" asked Beanie.

Fields said, "DNA found at the scene wasn't a match for Charles Ward. Ballistics report showed Michelle was killed with a .38. Charles Ward bought a .22."

Beanie wasn't surprised. Janvier's suspicions had been unfounded, based on circumstantial evidence. The purchase of a gun and the absence of an alibi could cause doubt, sure. But without a ballistics report or DNA to support Charles Ward's presence at the crime scene, it had been premature to charge the man with murder.

"Before I go, you remember that pack of drug-laced cigarettes the crime scene guys found in Eric Barnes' office?"

Opening a Word doc, Beanie said, "The medical examiner determined that the cigarettes killed Eric."

"Remember there were three sets of prints on the pack of

cigarettes," said Fields. "Eric Barnes' prints. Unknown male prints, and unknown female prints."

"Right," said Beanie, typing notes.

"Turns out, the unknown female prints belonged to Michelle Ward," Fields said. "Still no match on the unknown male prints."

Beanie leaned back in his chair. "What does Janvier think about Michelle's prints on the cigarette pack?"

"I think it blows a huge hole in his theory about Wanda Barnes," said Fields. "If she gave her husband the cigarettes, why aren't her prints on the cigarette pack?"

"Exactly," said Beanie, typing more notes.

"Janvier thinks Wanda was wearing gloves," said Fields. "He's still not ready to dismiss her as a suspect."

"Why am I not surprised?"

"Of course, I think Janvier is off base," said Fields. "Michelle might have had something to do with Eric Barnes' death. Her prints were on the cigarettes. And she had access to the new pain drug. Problem is, Vaughn Pharma is denying that any of the compound is missing. My hunch is that if Michelle did steal the drug, the company doesn't want it to get out in the public."

Beanie said, "Might affect whether or not the drug is approved, I would guess. I imagine people—and investors—might be leery if they knew an employee was able to steal a batch of the drug. Might make you wonder if Vaughn Pharma has sufficient security protocols in place to prevent theft and possible tampering."

"Agreed," said Fields. "Anyway, I'm thinking that unknown male DNA is key. Whoever that guy is gave Eric Barnes those cigarettes. That's the murderer."

After ending his conversation with Fields, Beanie went to the breakroom for a second cup of coffee. He grabbed a Styrofoam cup, and—

"Hey, been looking for you ..."

Turning, Beanie saw Stevie loping into the breakroom.

"What's up?" asked Beanie, grabbing a K-cup pod from the carousel.

"My cousin got more information from Eric Barnes' phone," said Stevie, grinning as he waved a manila file folder back and forth.

Beanie asked, "Something other than the threatening messages from Michelle Ward?"

Nodding, Stevie walked over to a table.

Setting his coffee to brew, Beanie joined Stevie.

"My cousin uncovered some deleted texts that Eric Barnes sent to a burner phone," said Stevie, opening the file.

"Was he able to find out who the burner belongs to?" asked Beanie.

Stevie glanced up at him. "Why do you always think my cousin is a guy?"

Resisting the urge to roll his eyes, Beanie said, "I meant to ask … was *your cousin* able to find out who the burner belongs to?"

"Unfortunately, no," said Stevie, removing documents from the files. "But these texts are very interesting. Take a look."

Beanie read the texts.

Eric Barnes: Been getting weird emails. Might be about that problem I took care of for you in St. Felipe last April

Unknown burner: Just ignore it

Eric Barnes: How did the guy get my name?

Unknown burner: Relax

Eric Barnes: Not going down for you

Unknown burner: Stop panicking

Eric Barnes: Think I need to get off this island. Go back to US

Unknown burner: Do what you think is best

Eric Barnes: I need money

Unknown burner: How much?

Eric Barnes: At least $100k

Unknown burner: I'll see what I can do

Eric Barnes: Get it done or else.

"What problem do you think Eric took care of in St. Felipe?"

Beanie looked up. "I don't know, but …"

"But what?" asked Stevie.

"Wanda told me that Eric took several trips to St. Felipe last April," said Beanie. "Now I'm wondering if his trips had something to do with the problem he handled for this unknown person."

"Any idea who the unknown person could be?"

Glancing at the texts again, Beanie picked up on the confrontational tone. Landon George's claim that Eric had argued with another man at Dizzy Jenny's floated into his mind. Was the man who'd contended with Eric the same person who sent messages from the unknown burner phone?

"No idea," said Beanie. "But it's interesting that Eric mentions the weird emails."

"You think those are the emails Eric wanted you to check out?"

Nodding, Beanie said, "I have a feeling he was referring to the coolkidstable email."

Stevie frowned. "You still think coolkidstable dude is Melvin Reed's son?"

"I think I need to talk to Oscar Reed," said Beanie. "First, I need to find him."

44

"My dad was being threatened by a former business partner," said Oscar Reed, a slight, skinny kid dressed in a well-fitting light-colored seersucker suit.

Sitting on a bench in a small park near the St. Killian library, Beanie glanced at Melvin Reed's son.

After learning about the deleted texts on Eric Barnes' phone, Beanie reached out to Ash, who promised to ask a few of Oscar Reed's friends if they'd seen him. Three days ago, she'd called Beanie to tell him she'd found Oscar.

"I told him you were looking for him," said Ash. "I explained that you might have information about his dad. He wants to meet you."

With Ash's help, Beanie secured the meeting with Oscar Reed.

"Who was the business partner?" asked Beanie.

Oscar sighed. "I don't know. That's what I was trying to find out."

"Wait," said Beanie. "How did you know your dad was being threatened?"

"After my dad was killed," said Oscar, "I got an invoice from a private investigator. Apparently, dad thought someone was following him. He was killed before he could pay the invoice. The private investigator told me that a guy named Eric Barnes was snooping around dad's house and stalking him. The private investigator gave me Eric Barnes' contact info, including his phone and email address."

"And you sent Eric Barnes the emails from the coolkidstable account?"

"I was too afraid to call the guy," said Oscar. "So I used Ash's computer to send Barnes the messages. I didn't want to spook Barnes, so I didn't confront him outright. I was hoping the messages would pique Barnes' interest and hopefully get Barnes to open up and maybe even meet with me. I just wanted to find out why Barnes was stalking my dad. Why he was following him?"

Beanie asked, "Did you think Eric Barnes knew the former business partner who was threatening your father?"

Oscar nodded. "I was hoping he'd tell me who the business partner was, but he didn't. Just like he didn't want to tell me what was bothering him the weeks before he died."

"And how did you know something was bothering your dad?" asked Beanie.

"Dad was acting strange," said Oscar, pinching the bridge of his nose. "Paranoid. Jumpy. Nervous. Wasn't like him. At first, he wouldn't tell me, but I kept questioning him. Eventually, he told me he'd been getting phone calls from someone telling him to stay quiet."

"Stay quiet about what?"

"He didn't want to tell me," said Oscar. "But I think it had something to do with one of his failed businesses. A tax accounting service. Dad told me he'd recently uncovered evidence that the tax service was being used to launder money."

"And you have no idea who your dad's former business partner could have been?" asked Beanie. "You didn't know any of the people he worked with?"

"My dad has had lots of businesses," explained Oscar. "Some of them failed, like the tax business. I didn't really know the partners he started the companies with."

Beanie rubbed his chin. "Did your father confront his former partner?"

"I don't know," said Oscar. "Dad told me he'd reached out to the island feds."

"He called the Palmchat Islands Investigative Bureau?"

Oscar nodded. "I don't know if dad ever met with anyone from the agency, though."

"Do you know how your father uncovered the evidence of money laundering?"

"He wouldn't tell me," said Oscar. "He didn't want to get me involved. After I found out about Eric Barnes, I wondered if maybe he knew something about the money laundering."

Snippets of the conversation with Lime Shoes floated into his head.

The gang had some questions for Barnes about a friend of his who, at the time, was under investigation by the PIIBs ... this friend had once laundered money for the gang ...

Beanie asked, "Did Eric Barnes ever contact you?"

Exhaling, Oscar shook his head. "Never. And now that Eric Barnes is dead, I'll never know if he knew anything about what happened to my dad, or not."

"I believe Eric Barnes knew about the money laundering," said Beanie. "I think he knew who threatened your dad. I think the same person who threatened your father killed Eric Barnes. And I think ..."

Oscar frowned. "You think ... what?"

One of the deleted texts Stevie's hacker cousin had uncovered flashed through Beanie's mind: *Might be about that problem I took care of for you in St. Felipe*

Beanie said, "I think Eric Barnes killed your father."

45

Beanie took a sip of the Felipe beer he'd been nursing for the past few hours and glanced at his wife. "So … what do you think?"

Leaning back in the lawn chair, Noelle sighed. "I can't believe Eric Barnes killed Melvin Reed."

As their boys ran around in the backyard, playing "cops and robbers," Beanie relaxed with Noelle on the patio. Three days had passed since Beanie's conversation with Oscar Reed, Melvin's son. In that time, Beanie had tried to prove his theories, with little success, until he'd spoken with Vivian this morning.

The Managing Editor had a secret contact with the PIIBs who'd confirmed Beanie's suspicions, which he'd spent the afternoon sharing with Noelle.

"Well, Vivian's contact confirmed it," said Beanie, recalling the conversation, which had taken place in the conference room. Vivian had called the contact on a secure line. The disembodied voice had been slightly distorted so that Beanie hadn't been able to discern if a man, or a woman, was speaking. Hadn't mattered, though. Beanie had only been interested in the information the contact had imparted.

After discovering that his former partner, whose name the contact refused to tell them, had used their business to launder money, Melvin Reed contacted the PIIBs.

Beanie said, "The island feds don't just jump when someone brings them a tip, however. There is serious vetting of the information before they begin an investigation. The PIIBs were still in the vetting stage when Melvin Reed was killed last year, in April."

"What did the feds think when Melvin was killed?" asked Noelle.

Letting out a loud whoop, Ethan chased a giggling Evan around a palm tree. After calling to the boys to be careful as they horsed around, Beanie said, "They started looking more seriously into his allegations against his partner, especially when they learned that Melvin Reed had contacted the local St. Felipe police about being followed."

"How did the partner find out that Melvin Reed went to the feds?"

"Vivian's contact said the feds believe a PC-5 mole in their organization tipped off the gang," said Beanie. "Then the cartel leaned on the partner. I'm thinking that's when the former partner decided to kill Melvin Reed. So the former partner paid Eric Barnes to commit murder."

Noelle sipped her beer, then said, "So how did Oscar find out about Eric Barnes?"

Beanie said, "When Oscar Reed learned that his father had hired a private investigator who'd learned Melvin Reed was being stalked by a man named Eric Barnes, Oscar reached out to Barnes, emailing him from the coolkidstable account, hoping for answers about his father's death."

"But Oscar never got the answers from Eric," said Noelle.

Shaking his head, Beanie said, "I think Eric reached out to the business partner—"

"And you think the business partner is the 'Unknown Burner' in the deleted texts on Eric's phone?"

"Right," confirmed Beanie. "I think Eric threatened the business partner. He sent a text demanding money."

"The business partner didn't give Eric any money, though," said Noelle.

Beanie sighed. "I think the business partner gave Eric a drug-laced cigarette instead."

46

"I think I know who was threatening Melvin Reed," said Beanie, standing in the copy room with Sophie, who was using the scanner.

"Who?" asked Sophie, pressing the buttons on the machine's built-in keypad. "And how did you find out?"

Leaning against the copy machine, Beanie folded his arms. "I did some research on Melvin Reed. Turns out, the tax accounting firm was a partnership between him, and a guy named Edward Collins."

"You think this Edward Collins guy paid Eric Barnes to kill Melvin Reed?" asked Sophie.

Beanie nodded. "Yeah, I do. And if Melvin Reed contacted the PIIBs about Edward Collins, then—"

"Then your theory might be right," said Sophie, feeding documents into the scanner. "Have you tried to contact Edward Collins?" asked Sophie.

Sighing, Beanie said, "I haven't been able to find a good number for him."

"Maybe you should contact Wanda Barnes," suggested Sophie.

Rubbing his chin, Beanie said, "You think she knows Edward Collins?"

"It's possible. If Eric and Edward Collins were arguing at Dizzy Jenny's, then obviously they were acquaintances. Wanda might know the guy because Eric mentioned him, or introduced him to Wanda," said Sophie.

"Why would Eric introduce his wife to the man who'd paid him to kill Melvin Reed?"

With an exasperated sigh, Sophie threw up her hands. "Or, if she doesn't, maybe she could find his contact info for you. I'm thinking Eric Barnes probably wouldn't have the guy's number in his phone, but maybe he had an address book."

"Maybe." Beanie shrugged. "Might be worth a shot."

Moments later, back at his desk, Beanie placed a call to Wanda Barnes.

"Mrs. Barnes, this is Roland Bean," he said when Wanda answered. "I don't want to take up too much of your time, but I was wondering if I could ask you something …"

"Only if you'll return the favor and allow me to ask you something," she said.

"Why don't you go first," suggested Beanie.

"Have you learned anything else about Eric's murder case?" she asked. "I mean, other than the fact that Detective Janvier still believes that I killed my husband."

"You know about the fingerprints on the pack of cigarettes the cops found, right?" asked Beanie, trying to determine if she'd read his story, **POLICE CONNECT SLAIN SCIENTIST TO EVIDENCE RELATED TO PAIN DRUG VICTIM.**

"I'm not surprised that Michelle Ward had something to do with Eric's murder," said Wanda. "I tried to tell that idiot Janvier. Those threatening texts from Michelle didn't convince him. Why should physical evidence change his mind?"

"Well, I haven't heard anything else from the police," said Beanie, deciding not to tell Wanda his theory about Edward Collins hiring Eric to kill Melvin Reed.

"Then what did you want to ask me?"

Beanie cleared his throat. "Did you know if Eric had a friend or acquaintance named Edward Collins?"

"Edward Collins?" echoed Wanda. "The name doesn't sound familiar, but Eric had a lot of friends I didn't know. Most of them, he met before we were married."

Disappointed, Beanie said, "Did Eric have an address book he kept around the house?"

"Not that I know of," said Wanda. "He kept contact numbers in his phone. But maybe you could talk to some of his friends you met at the party. Aaron, Ted, or Keith might have heard of Edward Collins."

47

"Thanks for agreeing to meet with me," said Beanie, stepping into the foyer of Ted's Adagio Bay condo.

"No problem." Ted closed the door. "We can talk in the living room."

Moments later, Beanie sat down on the couch across from the chair where Ted took a seat.

"On the phone," began Ted, "you said you had questions about an acquaintance of Eric's?"

Beanie nodded. "A man named Edward Collins."

Ted looked thoughtful. "Edward Collins?"

"Does the name ring a bell?" asked Beanie.

"No, I'm afraid not," said Ted. "Did you ask Wanda?"

"She suggested that I ask you, Aaron, and Keith," said Beanie, fighting to temper his disappointment. "I spoke to them already. Neither of them recognized the name."

Ted sighed. "You know, Eric had lots of friends. Most of them I didn't know. Sorry I can't be of more help."

Sighing, Beanie said, "I was just hoping to find this guy because I think he killed Eric."

"Do you have proof you can take to the cops?" asked Ted.

"Not exactly," admitted Beanie. "I have a theory that will be hard to prove unless I can talk to Edward Collins and maybe trick him into incriminating himself."

"Why do you think Edward Collins killed Eric?"

"Edward Collins once owned a tax accounting service with a man named Melvin Reed," said Beanie. "I believe Reed found out that Collins was using the business to launder money, so he contacted the PIIBs. Somehow, Collins found out and hired Eric Barnes to kill Reed. Then Eric tried to extort money from Collins, so Collins killed Eric."

"Wow," exclaimed Ted, scratching his eyebrow. "That is a very sordid tale."

"One I think is true," said Beanie.

"But, if you can't prove it," said Ted.

"As I said," Beanie told him, "I'm hoping to find Edward Collins and question him."

"And you think he's going to admit his guilt to you?" asked Ted. "You might not be able to trick him into confessing."

"I have to try," said Beanie. "And I'm thinking that if Edward Collins is found, his prints will be a match for the unknown male prints on the pack of cigarettes the police found in Eric's office. And the DNA from the shoe found at Michelle Ward's house will match Collins' DNA."

Ted rubbed his jaw. "So, you think that this … Edward Collins … killed Michelle, too?"

Beanie nodded. "It'll be hard to prove, but I think Michelle provided the pain drug to Edward Collins, who put it into a cigarette and gave it to Eric Barnes."

"Interesting," said Ted. "But, as you said, I doubt you'll be able to prove any of this and I don't even think you should waste your time trying to prove vague theories and speculation."

Beanie frowned. "These are not vague theories. I truly believe that—"

"I thought you were going to stop smoking!"

Beanie jumped, though he recognized the voice. Turning his head, he wasn't surprised to see Beverly, Ted's young, buxom redhead girlfriend. Strutting across the living area in short shorts, a crop top, and high-heel sneakers, she scowled as she stalked up to Ted.

"Bev, please," said Ted, frowning as he stood. "Can we discuss this later? Mr. Bean and I are in the middle of a conversation."

"And I was in the middle of writing an essay for my class when I opened the desk drawer to look for a pen and found a pack of cigarettes!" said Bev, hands on her hips. "And I wasn't even surprised! I knew you'd lied to me about the smoking!"

Ted sighed. "I know, sweetheart, but—"

"You promised me you would stop smoking," said Bev, crossing her arms.

"Beverly, please—"

"Don't you Beverly me, Edward!" scolded Bev.

As Ted placated the young woman with soothing promises, an icy chill passed through Beanie. Bev had called Ted … *Edward.* Beanie's heart pounded. Ted's name was Edward? Beanie didn't know what to think. Except … the man who might have killed Eric Barnes and Michelle Ward was named Edward. Only that man's last name was Collins. Ted's last name was Clark.

And yet … Beanie wasn't sure what he was thinking. The direction of his thoughts seemed to be leading him to a strange question. One that didn't make sense, but—

"I don't want to be here right now!" Bev pouted. "I'm going to the library to finish my paper."

"Honey, please, don't—"

"Shut up!" Bev shouted as she stomped toward the foyer. "I'm sick of your lies!"

Seconds later, the front door slammed with a resounding crash, sending a tremoring vibration throughout the living room.

Ted exhaled, then sank back down onto the sofa. "Sorry about that.

Bev throws tantrums. Not much difference between her and a two-year-old."

Beanie glanced at Ted. "Your name is Edward?"

Ted cleared his throat. "Edward is my given name, but I've always gone by Ted."

"Oh … " said Beanie, feeling like a rube. "Of course."

Ted was a nickname for Edward. Beanie knew that, and yet—

Beanie's gaze dropped toward the coffee table. A memory invaded his mind. The last time Bev had interrupted his conversation with Ted, she'd thrown a deck shoe made of neon green canvas.

Ted said, "As I was saying … "

In Beanie's mind, the deck shoe on the coffee table segued into the shoe he'd seen at Michelle Ward's yard. The shoe he'd thought was familiar but wasn't sure about. The shoe with traces of Michelle's blood and the killer's DNA.

"Mr. Bean?"

Beanie glanced at Ted. "Um … I should probably get going."

"You know, I was thinking about the man you're looking for … Edward Collins," began Ted.

Apprehensive, Beanie asked, "What about him?"

"I might know how to find him," said Ted, standing. "There's an old contact of Eric's you should probably reach out to. His contact information is on a business card in my office. Let me get it for you."

As Ted disappeared out of the living room and around a corner, Beanie took a breath, pulled out his phone. Hands shaking slightly, he sent texts to Officer Fields, Vivian, and his coworkers at the Palmchat Gazette. *I'm with Ted Clark at his condo in Adagio Bay. I think he killed Eric Barnes. I'll explain when I get back to the office. Leaving now.*

Pushing his phone into the pocket of his trousers, Beanie stood and hurried toward the door. Ted would be shocked when he returned and found him gone, but Beanie didn't care. He wasn't going to spend another minute with a man he suspected had killed two people. At the door, Beanie grabbed the knob and—

"Leaving so soon?"

A shudder passed through Beanie. Cursing under his breath, he sighed. There was no need to worry. Or be afraid. He'd just tell Ted he got an urgent call from his boss about breaking news. After a quick exhale, Beanie turned and—

"Thought you wanted to find Edward Collins?" asked Ted.

Beanie's gaze dropped from Ted's snarl to the gun in the man's hand.

Raising his hands, Beanie said, "I think I've already found him."

Ted scoffed. "Is that right?"

"You're Edward Collins, aren't you?" asked Beanie.

His expression smug, Ted said, "My name is Edward Clark … Collins."

Recalling the housekeeper who'd referred to Ted as Mr. Collins, Beanie looked away from the gun. "And you killed Eric Barnes and Michelle Ward?"

Ted laughed. "Mr. Bean, I think that's pretty obvious."

"So … what's the plan?" asked Beanie. "You've got a gun. I've got my hands up …"

"I'll admit I'm not quite sure," said Ted. "Wasn't exactly expecting this, so…"

"Well, while you're trying to come up with something," said Beanie, "why don't we talk about my vague theories?"

Ted shrugged. "Not exactly interested in that conversation."

Beanie took a breath. He wasn't interested in having the conversation, either. Beanie just needed to keep the man talking until he could figure out some way to escape.

"Well, it's just the two of us here," said Beanie. "We can talk freely. No one will know the truth."

"Except your readers," said Ted. "I expect you to write a heck of a story featuring my confession."

Beanie scoffed. "I don't think my readers will ever know about your confession."

Ted looked confused. "What do you mean?"

"Don't you plan to kill me?" asked Beanie, lowering his hands. "If so, I'd like to know if I was right about you before I die."

Ted rubbed his eyes with his free hand. "Yeah, I don't know …"

"What don't you know?" Beanie snaked a hand behind his back and grabbed the door handle.

Chuckling, Ted shook his head. "I don't know how you figured it all out."

"So you did kill Eric and Michelle?"

"Didn't exactly have a choice," said Ted. "After Eric killed Melvin Reed—"

"Guess I was right about that, too," said Beanie, slowly turning the knob.

"Melvin turned me into the PIIBs," said Ted. "For something I did two years ago at a company that went out of business."

"Two years ago?" asked Beanie, debating his next move. He could only think to quickly twist the knob, open the door, and run out of the house. And hope and pray that Ted would be caught off guard. "Why did Melvin want to turn you in if the company was out of business?"

"Melvin was always suspicious about why the company failed," said Ted. "I'd given him a story about a downturn in the number of clients, but I don't think he ever believed me. The truth was that the PC-5 wanted me to close up shop."

"Why?"

"They got a tip that the local cops were suspicious of the business," said Ted. "Anyway, Melvin started snooping around and found out some things he shouldn't have. Things he went to the PIIBs about."

"Wouldn't the statute of limitations have run out by then?"

Ted said, "I wasn't worried about the statute of limitations. I was worried about the PC-5. The money laundering was on their behalf. Once the PIIBs learned that, they would try to flip me."

"I don't think you'd be stupid enough to snitch on the gang," said

Beanie, hesitating. He was anxious to make his move. And apprehensive about getting shot in the back.

"Of course, I wouldn't," said Ted. "But that wouldn't matter. The PC-5 would kill me anyway because I got caught."

"So after Eric killed Melvin, what happened?" asked Beanie, grasping the doorknob with damp fingers.

"Eric told me he started getting threatening emails from someone," said Ted. "He started panicking. Saying he wanted money."

"Eric was blackmailing you," said Beanie.

"Wasn't exactly blackmail," said Ted. "He never threatened to go to the cops. And I didn't think he would because he would have brought suspicion on himself."

"So why kill him?"

"Because I didn't want to give him any more money," said Ted. "I'd already given him enough cash to buy that house in Oyster Farms. And I was worried about those emails. Worried that someone would find out Eric had killed Melvin and that person would go to the police. Figured it would be best if Eric was no longer around to answer any questions."

Beanie asked, "And Michelle Ward helped you kill Eric?"

"Got the pain drug from her," said Ted. "Rolled the cigarettes myself and gave them to Eric. He'd started secretly smoking and didn't want Wanda to know. He was happy to get the cigarettes. Didn't suspect a thing."

"Tell me something …" Beanie tried to twist the knob, but his hand slipped. "Did Michelle know you were going to kill Eric?"

Ted scoffed. "Why do you think she gave me the pain drug? She wanted him dead. With his testimony against her, she was going to lose those kids."

"And I'm guessing Michelle threatened to go to the cops, so you killed her?"

"Michelle wasn't going to go to the cops," said Ted. "Why would she? If she told the cops about me, I'd tell the cops about her. If she tried to take me down, then she'd go down."

Repositioning his hand, trying to grip the slippery doorknob, Beanie asked, "So, why did you kill her?"

"Out of an abundance of caution," said Ted.

"An abundance of caution?"

"Michelle was a loose end," said Ted. "It was only a matter of time before the cops traced the pain drug back to her. Only a matter of time before the police figured out, someway, that she'd given the cigarettes to Eric. And what do you think she would do if that happened?"

Beanie said, "She would have told the police that—"

Something blunt and hard slammed against the small of Beanie's back. He pitched forward, stumbling to his knees.

"I forgot my—" Beverly's voice died.

Ted cursed.

"Oh my God, Ted!" yelled Beverly as she stomped into the house. "What are you doing with that gun?"

His heart slamming, Beanie scrambled to his hands and knees. "He's getting ready to kill me with it."

Beverly looked at Beanie. "What? Kill you? Why would he do that?"

"Because he killed Eric Barnes and Michelle Ward," said Beanie. "And he doesn't want me to tell the cops."

Gasping, Beverly turned and walked toward Ted. "Is he serious? Did you kill Eric and Michelle?"

"Get back!" growled Ted, pointing the gun at Beverly.

The young redhead stopped in her tracks. "What is your problem? Are you really pointing that gun at me right now? What? Are you going to shoot me?"

"Not unless you do exactly what I tell you," said Ted, taking a few steps backward.

"And what exactly are you going to tell me to do?" demanded Beverly.

"Go into my home office," instructed Ted. "Get my passport, and—"

"Your passport?" Beverly shrieked. "Why? Where are you going?"

"Beverly, just—"

"I will not!" announced Beverly as she stalked up to Ted. "Put the gun down before you hurt someone!"

"Beverly, get back!" Ted shouted as Beverly tried to grab the gun from him. "I don't want to hurt you! Don't make me shoot you!"

Struggling with Ted, Beverly said, "If you shoot me, I'll kill you!"

Confused and terrified, Beanie decided to make a move. Ted and Beverly stumbled across the living room, fighting for control of the gun, their movements jerky and chaotic.

Beanie rushed toward Ted. Crouching low, he rammed his shoulder against Ted's side, putting every ounce of his weight into the blow. Off-balance, Ted staggered, becoming entangled with Beverly, and dropped the gun. It clattered across the floor as Ted cursed, demanding that Beverly get off him. Beanie lunged for the gun, grabbed it, and staggered to his feet.

Facing Ted and Beverly, who seemed to be finding it difficult to extricate themselves from one another, Beanie struggled to breathe.

"Don't you move!" Beanie ordered, pointing the gun at Ted.

"Do I look like I can move!" Ted said.

"You crazy old jerk!" cried Beverly. "Get away from me!"

"Gladly!" retorted Ted.

Walking backward, the gun in his right hand still trained on Ted, Beanie reached a trembling hand into his pocket. He pulled out his phone. Beanie continued to walk backward until he was in the foyer. There he placed the gun on a side table and called the police.

EPILOGUE

"You promised you wouldn't put yourself in danger anymore …"

Beanie glanced at Noelle, sitting next to him on a bench in the small Oyster Farms neighborhood park where they watched Ethan and Evan horse and clown around with several other kids on the playground.

Shielding his eyes from the late afternoon sun, Beanie sighed. "I know and I didn't mean to put myself in danger, but—"

"But you almost got shot," said Noelle.

"But I didn't get shot," said Beanie. "And I didn't know I was putting myself in danger. I had no idea that Ted Clark was really Edward Collins."

"I know, I know," said Noelle. "Speaking of Ted … I assume he's heading to Tiverton."

Beanie scoffed. "That's the last place he probably wants to go. The PC-5 might not make things easy for him in prison, especially since I heard he's trying to flip on the gang to avoid jail time."

"The cartel will probably tell my father to kill Ted," said Noelle, looking away.

His stomach twisting, Beanie said, "Babe, I didn't mean to bring up your dad—"

"You didn't bring him up," said Noelle. "I did. And you know it's true. Josue Chartres went from executing the Death List to carrying out the Snitch List."

"The Snitch List?" asked Beanie, not quite sure what his wife was referring to. "What is that?"

"Not all snitches make the Death List," said Noelle. "Those who end up in prison get taken out by my dad and his thugs."

"Who told you that?"

Shaking her head, Noelle said, "I don't want to talk about it. Let's just hope Ted gets what he deserves."

"Life behind bars for arranging the murder of Melvin Reed," said Beanie, determined to respect his wife's wishes to avoid conversation about her father, the notorious cartel hitman. "And for killing Eric Barnes and Michelle Ward. Although, it's hard to feel any sympathy toward Eric, who killed an innocent man, or Michelle, who supplied Ted with the drugs to kill Eric."

"Is there any proof of Michelle's involvement other than her fingerprints on the pack of cigarettes?" asked Noelle.

Beanie said, "Turns out, the security department at Vaughn Pharma knew she'd stolen fentanyl and samples of the new pain drug from the company."

"And they didn't fire her? Didn't have her arrested?"

Sighing, Beanie said, "From what Fields said, the company viewed Michelle Ward as a valuable asset, despite her sticky fingers. Apparently, Vaughn Hines was willing to overlook her transgressions because he stands to make billions on the new pain drug."

Noelle shook her head. "Why am I not surprised? I've heard he's a super shady guy with a very questionable moral compass."

"He wanted Michelle on the team developing that pain drug," said Beanie. "She was no use to him if she was in jail."

"Tell me, is Janvier finally ready to admit he was wrong about Wanda Barnes?" asked Noelle.

Chuckling, Beanie said, "I doubt it, but he has no choice. The evidence against Ted is overwhelming. His DNA was found in Michelle Ward's car and in the shoe he accidentally ran out of and left behind. All of that puts him at the crime scene. His fingerprints turned out to be a match for the unknown male prints found on the drug-laced cigarette given to Eric Barnes. And Vivian's PIIB contact confirmed that Melvin Reed came to them with information about Ted—or, should I say, Edward Clark Collins."

"What about the gun used to kill Michelle?"

"That was the same gun Ted pulled on me," said Beanie.

"Oh, don't remind me," said Noelle.

Beanie decided to change the subject somewhat. "The only good thing is that Oscar Reed finally knows what happened to his dad. Did I tell you about the gun Wanda found hidden in the laundry room? The one she said Eric used for target practice?"

"Was that the gun used to kill Melvin?"

Beanie nodded. "Ballistics report confirmed it."

Noelle said, "This whole situation with Eric, Ted, and Michelle is so awful and terrible. Just makes you wonder about people, you know?"

"Yeah, well, you never really know about people," said Beanie, rubbing his jaw.

Noelle said, "No, I suppose you don't, but—"

"Mommy! Mommy!"

Beanie smiled as Ethan and Evan ran toward them.

"Evan has to potty, Mommy!" announced Ethan. "Evan has to potty!"

Laughing under his breath, Beanie shook his head.

"You have to potty?" asked Noelle as Evan ran to her and grabbed her knees.

"Evan have to potty!" said Evan, giggling. "Evan have to potty!"

"Let's hope he really does have to potty," said Beanie, standing.

As Noelle reached down to pick up Evan, she glanced over her shoulder and asked, "Why do I get the feeling that he just wants to flush the toilet?"

Did you figure out who killed Eric and how he was killed?

There were a lot of suspects and even more sinister secrets to uncover but once Beanie figured out all the deadly motives, he discovered the killer.

Thanksgiving brought more mayhem than giving thanks for bountiful blessings and the 4th of July will bring even more dangerous sparks into Beanie's life.

Happy 4th of July Murder is the next holiday cozy murder mystery novel in the Reporter Roland Bean Cozy Mystery Series. It's guaranteed to bring even more twists and turns to keep you guessing until the shocking ending.

Get your copy of Happy 4th of July Murder today!
https://geni.us/happy4thofjulymurder

Are you eagerly anticipating Beanie's next unexpected detour into a mystery waiting to be solved?

Then **Beanie's Mini Mystery Moments** are for you!

Get an exclusive quick-read mystery that spins off from one of Beanie's mystery adventures delivered straight to your email inbox!
https://BookHip.com/TMKGBHQ

ALSO BY RACHEL WOODS

SASSY SARCASTIC CAT COZY MYSTERIES

Sophie Carter, a struggling reporter for the *Palmchat Gazette*, teams up with a sassy talking Calico cat to solve crimes as she strives to become an influential investigative reporter

A SLY AND SINISTER TAIL

A COLD AND CALCULATING TAIL

A FOUL AND FRIGHTENING TAIL

A DARK AND DEVIOUS TAIL

REPORTER ROLAND BEAN COZY MYSTERIES

Roland "Beanie" Bean, husband and loving father, finds himself the unwitting participant in solving crimes as he seeks to make a name for himself as a reporter for the *Palmchat Gazette*.

HAPPY BIRTHDAY MURDER

EASTER EGG HUNT MURDER

MERRY CHRISTMAS MURDER

TRICK OR TREAT MURDER

GOBBLE GOBBLE MURDER

HAPPY 4TH OF JULY MURDER

SUMMER VACATION MURDER

HAPPY NEW YEAR MURDER

PALMCHAT ISLANDS MYSTERIES

Married journalists, Vivian and Leo, manage the island newspaper while solving crimes as they chase leads for their next story.

UNTIL DEATH DO US PART

NO ONE WILL FIND YOU

YOU WILL DIE FOR THIS

DON'T MAKE ME HURT YOU

THE PALMCHAT ISLANDS MYSTERIES BOX SET: BOOKS 1 - 4

RUTHLESS REVENGE ROMANCE SERIES

Gripping romantic suspense series with steamy romance, unpredictable plot twists and devastating consequences of deceit.

HER DEADLY MISTAKE

HER DEADLY DECEPTION

HER DEADLY THREAT

HER DEADLY BETRAYAL

MURDER IN PARADISE SERIES

A series of stand-alone women sleuth mysteries with murder, mayhem and a dash of romance, set against the backdrop of turquoise waters and swaying palm trees of the fictional Palmchat Islands.

THE UNWORTHY WIFE

THE SILENT ENEMY

THE PERFECT LIAR

ABOUT THE AUTHOR

Rachel Woods studied journalism and graduated from the University of Houston where she published articles in the Daily Cougar. She is a legal assistant by day and a freelance writer and blogger with a penchant for melodrama by night. Many of her stories take place on the islands, which she has visited around the world. Rachel resides in Houston, Texas with her three sock monkeys.

For more information:
www.therachelwoods.com
rachel@therachelwoods.com

ABOUT THE PUBLISHER

BONZAIMOON BOOKS

BonzaiMoon Books is a family-run, artisanal publishing company created in the summer of 2014. We publish works of fiction in various genres. Our passion and focus is working with authors who write the books you want to read, and giving those authors the opportunity to have more direct input in the publishing of their work.

For more information:
www.bonzaimoonbooks.com
info@bonzaimoonbooks.com